Five New Facts About Giorgione

With best wishes to
Leo Mc Donough
from the author
October 17th
1990.

Hugh Herd

Also by Hugh Hood

NOVELS

White Figure, White Ground
The Camera Always Lies
A Game of Touch
You Can't Get There From Here

THE NEW AGE / LE NOUVEAU SIÈCLE

The Swing in the Garden
A New Athens
Reservoir Ravine
Black and White Keys
The Scenic Art
The Motor Boys in Ottawa
Tony's Book

STORIES:

Flying a Red Kite
Around the Mountain: Scenes from Montréal Life
The Fruit Man, the Meat Man, and the Manager
Dark Glasses
Selected Stories
None Genuine Without This Signature
August Nights

NON-FICTION:

Strength Down Centre: The Jean Béliveau Story
The Governor's Bridge Is Closed
Scoring: Seymour Segal's Art of Hockey
Trusting the Tale

Five New Facts About Giorgione

Hugh Hood

Black Moss Press

Financial assistance towards publication
of this book was provided by
the Canada Council and
the Ontario Arts Council.

Black Moss books are distributed by Firefly Books,
3520 Pharmacy Avenue, Unit 1-C,
Scarborough, Ontario M1W 2T8.
All orders should be directed there.

Cover: Hugh Hood

PRINTED AND BOUND IN CANADA
AT COACH HOUSE PRESS, TORONTO

ISBN 0 88753 155 5

For Judith Fitzgerald

one

THE NAG'S HEAD FEATURED FROSTED GLASS on the mirrors behind the bars, on the gleaming panels set into the swinging doors of the entryway and as decoration on the tall foggy partitions which separated a series of stalls arranged for the use of small groups of drinkers who liked to remain apart from the jolly crowds of cocktail time, to pursue conversations limited to two or three participants. These booths had not proved popular with the late afternoon crowds; the proprietors had for some time considered getting rid of them. At the same time there were about twenty habitués of the Nag's Head who seemed to enjoy the qualified isolation conferred by the tall icy panels, the solid backs of the facing benches, the illusion of hoary antiquity conveyed by the weighty oak-veneer tables which stood in each cubicle.

These folk were eaters as well as drinkers, were stayers who might be coaxed into becoming regular diners. This traditional English pub, while not obliged to observe the constricted hours of business of the European original, here sought to introduce the *cut off the joint and two veg* kind of dining which had stayed so many British stomachs over the generations. The Nag's Head didn't have to shut down in early afternoon and open up in the early evening; it stayed open the whole time and actively promoted cut-price dining and its privilege of remaining open until very late. Some thought too late. The pub was a little goldmine located (surprisingly) between Walker and Woodlawn on Yonge. There, goldmines are few.

Neil Tarrant, like other regulars, now verged upon creating in the Nag's Head a little home-from-home handy to his flat around the corner on Walker Avenue, one-third of an enormous brown brick early twentieth-century detached villa, much verandaed and

7

gabled, with the characteristic sprouting Toronto dormers and many traces of the cavernous heating systems of 1910 when Welsh blower coal was two dollars a ton. What kind of family could have projected and then actually inhabited that grandiose erection? His own suite of rooms was spacious enough for a modest family, though Neil enjoyed none of the pleasures and discharged none of the responsibilities of the family man. His flat comprised most of what had been the second floor together with an ingeniously arranged side entry. Two other persons held tenancy of longer or shorter leasehold in the other parts of the building: a young woman lived on the third floor, a young man on the ground floor. In certain ways, both made agreeable – even attractive neighbours.

Neil's apartment could readily have accommodated four to six persons perfectly. Two of his big bedrooms were never used by him for their designed purpose. The dining-room was likewise diverted to specialised ends. These three rooms were now hung on every wall and panel and in every corner with coloured and black-and-white reproductions – in every size including the largest – of the masterworks of Venetian painting of the great age, sometimes arranged in startling and illuminating sequences. A tiny detail of some immense work of genius, some head or torso or swag of drapery or shining work of jewellery, occupying an inconspicuous place in the magnificent original, might appear magnified successively in larger and larger sizes and in various ranges of colour or black-and-white.

The cumulative impression left by the three rooms as an observer moved from one to the next was that often produced by those eighteenth-century pictures of the artist in his studio in which crowds of finished canvasses are ranked in rows from floor to ceiling, some skied in unfortunate positions from which no true estimate of their value may be taken, others partly concealed under draperies or buried beneath objects connected with the artist's craft, a few reproduced in miniature renderings strikingly bright in hue, these generally the most saleable of the unsold works in the artist's stock.

8

The middle room of the three, once a large bedroom, contained a floor-to-ceiling mirror in which dozens of the reproductions on display were reflected. As a viewer moved from one side of the room to another, more and more of the pictures swam into view in the mirror, in dim evening light giving the place a subaqueous Proustian exoticism of atmosphere. Over the top of the mirror Neil had painted in large raggedly-formed green lettering a single word: ZORZON.

Across the room, facing this enigmatic scrawl, dashed briskly over the surfaces of five cheaply reproduced "Virgin and Child with Saints" pictures – favourite Venetian subject – in huge splashes of crimson could be seen the response: ZANZIAN. It was set out in the baby language of the lords of a quarter and half-a-quarter.

Very few people had been granted the privilege of inspecting this remarkable display of research material. Neil invited no colleagues to dine with him, never explained afterwards over coffee the intricacies of his investigations. He chose not to discuss them. There were certain natural traps embedded in the soft Venetian underpinnings of his work, in which you might readily drive deep piles, though these might later on bear less weight than had been hoped. The ground beneath his feet was swampy and marine, fever-ridden, appropriate for naval pursuits; some of these submarine enough in character, as secret as the wet dungeons of the Serenissima, into which little light was permitted to shine. No place on earth has been as much studied, perhaps, as the many-islanded lagoon; certainly none has evoked such ambiguous findings.

Neil went often to the Nag's Head to save himself the bother of cooking, the risk of smirching his rooms full of swirling colour with the smoke of frying grease. Women sometimes inquired whether they might come and prepare something for him. Was his apartment fitted with a cooker of any kind, a microwave or handy toaster oven? To these solicitations he would make no definite reply, preferring the simple refusal of kind attentions rendered by evasion and qualified lucidity. He would offer instead the hospitality of the local pub; he sometimes met his upstairs neighbour there after work. Such was the case this afternoon.

He sat, Neil Tarrant, scratching at the frosted panel beside him with an over-long cracked fingernail, wondering why the deposit of frosting came off so readily. It fell in a fine powder on the seat beside him. A border of ornament ran around the glass panels: acanthus leaves, palmettes, swags, the standard apparatus of beaux-arts pattern books, lions, horses. Who had put them there? He scratched and scratched, alone in his cubicle at 4:30, anxious for company, somebody to whom he might voice his discontents.

Why did the great Venetian painters have to have multiple names, or be one among crowds painting under the same name? Three Bellinis, a great one and two good ones. Why couldn't Tintoretto have been satisfied to remain simply Jacopo Robusto, roughly Jack Armstrong, an impressive enough name for even a very great painter. Why two Palmas, a really good one with a great love for plump blonde ladies and an adequate one without that pressing love? And why did Palma-of-the-blondes turn out not to be a Palma at all but a certain Jacopo Negreti, approximately Black Jake, whose birth date was at best uncertain? Why were they so elusive and approximate? Why did his own man, Big George, have to be the least proximate of all? (One day, a great authority had said, some new man will proclaim the purely mythical status of Big George, casting the provenance of ten of the most famous pictures in the world gravely in doubt.) What a life!

He had been giving a slide show for sophomores all afternoon, tripping them up again and again over their head-count of Guardis, not maliciously, simply as the consequence of the secretive, elusive, evasive, hopelessly knotted weave of connections which runs through the history of Venetian painting. Why not Paolo Caliari? Just because a chap comes from Verona, why does he have to proclaim the fact for 400 years? The men were as myth-ridden as their great works.

He would certainly have to pay a further visit to the master technician in the Louvre about that standing nude figure with jug in the *Fête Champêtre*. Careful x-ray study of the highlight on the bottom of the jug would unquestionably show three levels of treatment of the canvas in a sequence of underpainting, glazing, and highlighting as personally peculiar to the young Titian as his handwriting. The picture was wholly Titian's work and nobody else's. Neil was certain of this and, if his attribution were to stand, what would become of the ascription of *The Concert* in the Pitti? It was absolutely clear to him that the modelling of the head of the young man without a hat in the *Fête Champêtre*, with his straight firm nose and rounded, slightly receding chin, was identical with the rendering of the same skull, this time proposed as that of a middle-aged man with the same nose and chin in *The Concert*. The set of the head on the shoulders was the same; the form of the shadow under the jaw and left cheek was the same. Both pictures were by Titian and only by Titian, and the "Giorgionesque" qualities of both works were actually "Titianesque" in a singing and youthful tone which was that of the very young manhood of the master. Those persons who ascribed some part of either work to Big George from Castelfranco, whoever he might have been, were genuflecting before a ghost of their own creation, a striking instance of mass self-hypnosis.

"Why so glum, chum?"

And away into the recesses of his imagination went the whole fantastic structure of discovery, the slow remorseless chase across continents of the irrefutable evidence, the almost untraceable sinuous motion of a quarter-inch-long bit of underpainting, the blend of colour and clear oil in just exactly these proportions and no other, hints of almost invisible forms just barely accessible to intuition which might once have stood in fresco on the walls of the Fondaco dei Tedeschi, that torso, those hands. There was once upon a time a young man who came from Castelfranco to the lagoons, Zozo, Zorzo, Zorzon, who lived here and there, once bespoke Leonardo, may now and then have conversed with old Giovanni Bellini. Who died young. A songster. Courageous. Dark and handsome. May sometimes have held a brush.

All of this sank into the caverns and lagoons of his thoughts as he looked up at Betty Frits who stood in the doorway of the little dining cubicle in which he lounged unsatisfied – perhaps insatiable.

Behind her the sound of battle coursed along the bar; voices raised themselves in heated competition for the attention of young women. Not a singles bar exactly – certainly not the right spot for an easy pickup and in no way connected with any form of drug traffic – the Nag's Head more and more drew to itself crowds of young urban professionals; it might enjoy this status for another eighteen months. The phenomenon had declared itself more and more directly since the middle of 1984 when (for some infinitely obscure and undiscoverable reason) masses of persons earning from $60,000 to $100,000 a year began to come there. Young dentists who had specialised in orthodontia and now invested in Toronto-made horror films, magazine publishers who existed on Canada Council grants, Woodlawn Avenue broadcasting executives from the two radio stations up the street, and a third baseman and bride who chose to winter in the city during the off-season. They thought of themselves as the Lion Pride.

There was a softball team of that name: NAG'S HEAD LION PRIDE. Games took place on the Toronto islands, usually at Centre Island near one of the lagoons. The circumstance of there being lagoons and islands across Toronto Bay which formed in themselves a sandbar sequence of very Venetian type, with the Eastern Gap as a replica *porto di lido,* pleased Neil and had in part engendered his decision to remain in the city, to use it as his professional base.

Like Venice, Toronto was a city of lagoons and sandbars, and the light of the Canadian lake port, often watery and misty, smoky in September, bore a comparison not entirely absurd with the sacred light of the bride of the Adriatic. Cities of lagoons. The Toronto islands had been formed by silting and marine currents in precisely the same way as world-storied Venice and her lagoons had been formed by the outpourings of the Brenta, the Piave, the Sile.

"Why so glum, chum?" said Betty again. He focussed his dreaming eyes and saw her clear above him framed in the light, her speech filtered through the rousing competitive chorus by the softness and delicacy of her diction. Betty liked to keep her statements clear and void of ambiguity. She was his upstairs neighbour, a kind uninterfering woman of thirty who had been a liberal-arts major and, upon graduation, joined an upscale legal firm as a secretary. She had shown from the beginning an unquestionable gift for estate administration and after three years with the firm had taken her first steps towards a distinguished career. She specialised in nursing small estates into maximum safe-income yield. Nothing pleased her more than the regular payment of small but never insignificant quarterly earnings to testatees whose surprise and pleasure were her sole reward (apart from her very sizeable earnings). An unexpected dividend.

Betty's ambitions for the estates she babied and suckled were embedded in the notion of the prudent increases of property and earnings. As a benchmark she always tried to have the holdings of the given estate earn as much in a decade as would equal the sum available for investment, a consistent ten per cent at simple interest. If she placed $100,000 for the anguished widow or orphan, she hoped that these placements would yield a steady $10,000 a year so that, at the close of the first decade, the legatee would have received $10,000 in payments, all the while retaining the original sum intact. The miracle of capitalism. She could imagine no sweeter reward than the smile on the face of the testatee when the returns were totted up at the end of a decade. These actions were her form of charity, love of her fellows, participation in the human compact. Maybe one couldn't quite live on $10,000 yearly, but it was a hell of an income supplement and the capital remained intact; the earnings might be cumulated. Wow! Private enterprise.

Betty's opinion of paintings as long-term investment opportunities was low: There was no way to estimate the annual rate of appreciation, and there was the problem of obtaining an accurate baseline evaluation against possible capital-gains imposts. All you could do with a painting, she said, was look at it. There was no profit in self-improvement, presumably the object of aesthetic contemplation, and there was certainly no profit in mere raw pleasure. At the same time there was certainly something to be said for raw pleasure, if not for the self-improvement conferred by the – always questionable – moral aspect of the uses of bits of art. Anyway, who wants to be improved by studying painted pictures of painted ladies – surely a perverse method of cultivating an acute conscience?

Living downstairs to Betty Frits exposed Neil to many of her speculations on these and related subjects. She knew he was deeply into art; yet, she liked him and could see that he was by no means a fool. There was the vexing fact that on the whole the prices of many paintings – which ones? – tended to rise on a curve steeper than that of the general inflationary rise in all prices. In the 1920s you might at almost any time have encountered in Fitzrovia a man with a small Matisse or possibly a little Bonnard in his possession, perfectly genuine and the embodiment of his whole capital, which he would be prepared to sell for £400.

In the middle of the 1980s this same picture would carry so high a price that only oil sheikhs, stars in night-time TV serials, and baseball players could contemplate such a purchase. That kind of evolution of the priced into the priceless was what Betty Frits could not accept. There was a shift in the means of evaluation at work in such a development that would make any estate administrator bow his or her head in silent prayer. Value, value, what the hell!

Neil's university appointment was of unimpeachable dignity and authority. He was the coming young man in his field, Venetian painting of the high Renaissance, the associate of John Steer and Alastair Smart and Pierre de Chenonceaux and Gerhardt Duesterhaus. There was no subject in the history of modern European painting to which he was not in some sort adequate. He collected contemporary Canadian art in a small way. He never put his own collection into any visual relationship with the reproductions of masterpieces which furnished the three central rooms in his flat; rather, he kept his Canadian pieces in the kitchen, bathroom, and bedroom where they fitted right into his ordinary current of living. He meant no implied criticism of the "real" paintings which he owned; they just didn't go with the specimens hanging in colourful profusion in the three central rooms, his personal Accademia.

Neil's "real" collection of recent Canadian art, varied and fairly extensive (he owned about twenty works) was brilliantly chosen and constantly appreciating in value. He had bought these works at prices averaging around $600 so that his total holdings had cost him in the neighbourhood of $12,000 and were now worth twice that.

He couldn't have bought any of the objects pictured in his personal Accademia – not the very least of them – for less than $2,000,000.

Buy them young and buy them early!

"Got another evaluation for you to do," said Betty, sliding into the booth and sitting down across from him. She clutched a huge seidel of lager from which she ever and anon drew copious draughts. "One that you'll enjoy, an interesting collection."

"Where?"

"Up near the Hunt Club."

"Oh God, more Toronto Constables," said Neil. "That bugger Constable painted about 400 canvasses in his lifetime and over 600 of them are in Forest Hill and Mississauga."

"I didn't know that."

"Take it from me."

"Good fee though. It's a major estate this time." She dropped the name of a recently deceased speculator in grain futures.

"Is the wife living?"

"Is she not! She's the one who's arranging for the valuations. You'll like her; she knows all about art."

This was said with coy malice.

"You don't want me to suggest a potential valuation, not here, privately, sight unseen, in casual conversation?"

"Hell I don't," said Betty, flourishing her pot of drink.

"Do you want another of those?"

She emitted a lady-like belch. "Perhaps just one. Don't get up; let me go to the bar. Do you want anything?"

"Get me a half-litre of some rough Valpolicella to put me in the mood."

She vanished. There were shouts of recognition from a voice further along the bar. "Betty Frits, you old urban cowgirl, you. Here, little darlin', let me get those. Why shuckins, 'taint nuthin'."

Doesn't that man ever do any work, wondered Neil. He spends all his time here when he isn't over at the house listening to Kenny and Waylon. Hot damn!

Betty reappeared with the drinks, the huge form of Huey-Jack DuBoys looming behind her.

"Three Constables," said Betty to Neil, "two Girtins, a Cotman and an old Crome."

"And a parsnip in a pear-tree," hollered Huey-Jack. "What are you talking about, sweetheart?"

"I've got Neil doing some work for me."

"Is it anything Pappy could handle?"

"No, Huey-Jack, no, I don't reckon so."

"Willin' to make the effort. Why not set a spell and tell this ol' down-home country boy all about it?"

Neil started to gurgle with uncheckable laughter. When Huey-Jack got going on his Elmore Leonard / Burt Reynolds number there was little to do but relax and enjoy. At these times, Neil used to refer to the big fella as "Gator," a name which amused him almost out of his britches.

"Hey now, Gator," said Neil, "this ain't none of your business. I'm just gonna look at a few little ol' paintings for Missy, so don't sweat it, huh?"

"Paintings?"

"I might be able to edge your fee up a little," said Betty thoughtfully.

"Good idea," said Neil. "I'd been planning to up the rate. I presume we'll need a whole morning or afternoon to get it on?"

"Get what on?" asked Huey-Jack.

"Little business appointment, big guy."

"Aha. Oho."

"Now just a darn minute," said Betty, gathering her reputation around her.

"I'm just going to do an evaluation of some water-colours and an oil or two for current market value. Nuthin' for you there."

"Well I be dog," Huey-Jack shouted, "current market values are my meat, buddy. I eat 'em raw. They how I earn my grits. You wanna know what I did this morning?"

"If you want to tell us," said Betty, lifting an eyebrow in Neil's direction.

"Hell, sweetie-buns, ain't nuthin' to stop me, is there? You're gonna love this. I set the price on 4,500 service stations is all."

"Aw, go on!"

"Would I bullshit you? We're talking hundreds of millions of dollars here, and in them Canadian funny money coupons even; a hundred million dollars buys a stack of grits, lemme tell you."

"Oil," said Neil reverently.

"And government," said Betty.

"We're not talking some nelly-ass queen with shit on his Kodiaks and a swift line of nose candy. We're talkin' big big bucks and bottomless pockets."

"Your pockets and mine, citizen," said Betty.

"Shuckins, I ain't no citizen of this here little banana republic," said Huey-Jack in high good humour. This was a matter of public record. Never mind the false *bonhomie* and the Burt Reynolds facade, Huey-Jack DuBoys was a petroleum engineer with two advanced degrees in the field from the University of Tulsa, maybe the biggest oil university on earth. What he didn't know about world fossil-fuel reserves and markets wasn't even worth suspecting. He had started life as the manager of a string of drilling rigs which were partly owned by his father, a wanderer over the face of West Texas, Oklahoma, Alberta. In the mid-seventies, when the gross oil-pricing fiction had taken everybody in, Huey-Jack and his pappy had been hand-in-glove with the Getty gang in

Alberta. Drilling concessions flowed their way almost miraculously, unnaturally. There had been involvement with the Dome affair, then the Federal Conservatives had been thrust from power because they couldn't count up to 143, and PetroCan rose above the Canadian petroleum industry like an enormous monolith in Philistia or Canaan, sacred to the penis in any of several disguises, the bad towers of the Ba'als, notorious in Sacred Scripture. PetroCan became the Canadian symbol of independence; its flagged and bannered service stations had much to do with the decline of separatism in East and West. Soon PetroCan would range across the continent, a major retailer, a major producer. In 1984 Huey-Jack DuBoys and the DuBoys Explorations Group became first a wholly owned subsidiary of the state corporation; then the company name and its young executive vice-president disappeared into the maelstrom. Huey-Jack became national director of retail sales and distribution for the state-held agency. A terribly powerful man.

"What's 4,500 multiplied by $100,000?" asked Neil as he tried to make the calculation on a paper napkin.

"I can't do it, too many zeros," said Betty helplessly.

But Huey-Jack, armed with pocket calculator, gave the figure without hesitation.

"Real money," he said with satisfaction. "Somebody buy me a beer."

"Cheapskate," said Betty amiably. She left the booth in quest of further drink.

As soon as she had gone Huey-Jack leaned over to Neil and spoke confidentially.

"You got plans for the little lady?"

"You mean for tonight?"

"Or any night."

"Not tonight for sure. I sometimes work for her."

"Hey, Super-Stud, tell me about it."

"No way."

Betty rejoined them with fresh glasses and looked from one

18

man to the other. Her neighbours. It was imperative she remain on terms with both. She had plans for them. "I'll call you about the valuations," she said to Neil, "I think we can get together on a fee."

"What do they pay you for that kind of work?" asked Huey-Jack.

"It wouldn't interest you, big guy," said Neil. "A few hundred for half-a-day's work. All the same, I'm an authority."

"So am I an authority, but I don't do it for nuthin'. There can't be much call for your product, son."

"You'd be surprised," said a tightly smiling Neil.

"Venetian painting, ain't that right?"

"You got it."

"Cheese and crackers," said Huey-Jack, "I know everything there is to know about Venice. It's one of the biggest oil ports in the world, the key to European imports. Ain't you ever been in Mestre, son?"

"Never," said Neil with a shudder, "although I may just have passed through." He remembered the smell and the cancerous blight along the mainland shores of the lagoon.

"Buddy, they've got about a tenth of the refinery capacity of Europe right there. Place never shuts down, never gets dark; you can see the burnoff flares for fifty miles."

"I know," said Neil.

"That's Venice for you, right between the European capitals and the sheikhdoms, couldn't be better, holds the goddam gorgeous east in fee, am I right, son? You like Venice, old sport?"

"Yup."

"I'll give it to you for Christmas," said Huey-Jack, "you'd like that all right, wouldn't you?"

"I wouldn't take it as a gift," said Neil. "Nobody owns Venice, Gator, not even the oil companies. Venice is the centre of art history; there's more to be had out of Venice than oil. If I could discover five new facts about Giorgione I could rewrite modern history."

"Hey."

"No, I really could, because our understanding of the Renaissance is built on what we think of the springtime of Venetian painting."

"What's he smoking?" said Huey-Jack to Betty. "All those burrheads are finished and fading out. Ain't no reason why anybody gonna pay attention."

"Five information bits. That's all."

"Blow it out your floppy disk," said Huey-Jack inelegantly.

"If it all falls into place for me I can revise all the books. I can force everybody to see Bellini, Giorgione, Palma, and Sebastiano in a totally different light. That's what such a discovery implies."

"Whoo-ee," said Huey-Jack, blowing bubbles of foam across the table, "if'n that don't beat all. Shee-it!"

two

MESTRE SMELLED BAD. It often does and most of all on dank drizzling mid-winter afternoons. I should have come by sea the same way Jan Morris did, thought Neil. He had arrived in Venice by air several times, twice before by rail, but never from the sea which is the best of all ways to come to Venice, along the length of the Adriatic and through the Porto di Lido, across the narrow passage in the tricky deep-water channel past the Giudecca at last to the docks and the watery city shimmering in opalescent sunlight or withdrawing into antique dark. Arrival by rail, expedient for holders of Eurorail passes, is safe, quick, convenient, and dull dull dull. He felt this keenly and swore to himself as the wait in Mestre lengthened and the petroleum smells infiltrated his carriage, that this would be his last approach to Venice by rail. He glanced to his right at the long line of flaring lights in the shipyards, the industrial port, the refineries. The new Venice, the Venice of Huey-Jack DuBoys.

His exchange with Huey-Jack and Betty on the nature and value of research in art history was now several months behind him yet it lingered in the memory with a peculiar tang and smart. It seemed to Neil that his very reason for existing had been called into question. It was true, he conceded, that the old Venice of the lagoons had its own special odour of decay compounded of tidal silt, garbage, sewage, and the occasional corpse, which hung about the place like an invisible malarial miasma. The danger of fever was the inverse reciprocal of the extraordinary beauty of the place in all seasons. But the authentic Venetian odour of infectious decay was an eternity removed from the novel smell of the new mainland Venice. The train gave a lurch, stopped, lurched forward once more and moved slowly out onto the causeway. On the motorway next to the train a sparse parade of vehicles came and went, more of them headed west than east. Could the Venetians perhaps be stealing the automobiles of visitors and making for the Occident, quitting their islands for more salubrious places? A few commercial delivery vans were making a deliberate passage towards the enormous parking garage near the railway station which bars automobile traffic from "the heart of downtown Venice." Neil smiled grimly at the thought of the motorist in Venice baffled by the impossibility of bringing his car right to the centre of the picture postcards. It has often been suggested, not always by uncivilised tourists from North America, that the Grand Canal would make a splendid motorway if only the Soperintendenza would allow it to be filled in. One might then zip downtown from the end of the causeway to the Piazzetta in under five minutes, the whole damn island being no more than a couple of miles long from east to west and why not anyway? What's the point of barring automobile traffic?

Neil drowsed. The snail-like pace of the train began to lull him and the insult which Mestre seems to offer to antiquity began to seem less wounding than at first. Europe must have its oil; the big ships have to lie somewhere in the Lagoon. How soon would this damnable train be in the station?

He fell into a light doze and at once saw before him the face of M. de Chenonceaux, shadowed and saturnine, clean-shaven with hollow cheeks and the ruminative eyes of the profound scholar. They had sat deep in the underground stores of the Louvre, in a remote conference room equipped for very specialised scholarly labours, during four protracted afternoons of the previous week. In the room (besides their papers and a long table) were a slide projector of the most magnificent accuracy and efficiency, a screen, and trays and trays full of slides taken in every conceivable degree of light and shade. Slides of every square centimetre of the surface of the *Fête Champêtre,* slides most particularly of the left side of the painting which depicts the form of the beautiful nymph or maiden who dips her pitcher at the wellhead, the exquisite painterly modelling of the fingers and curved-under thumb of the right hand as she supports her weight on the top of the well. Most particularly of all, greatly magnified for close inspection, the slides of the pitcher or jug and of the highlighting which defines the curve of its form lay scattered for most of that week on top of the conference table, flashed one after another on the big screen for the critical examination of the celebrated *conservateur* and his young North-American confrère.

"I accept your conclusions," M. de Chenonceaux had finally declared. "You are about to project your researches into a grand unknown, indeed the grandest. Look here!" He cupped his hand imitatively beside the enlarged image of the pitcher which was projected on the screen. The cupped hand framed the dark semicircle which defines the bottom of the jug.

"Some of the cartoon is still visible, some of the first application of thinned black pigment. Beside it and overlying it there are a dozen glazes of colour on colour topped with that extraordinary smear of highlight, with the tiny dab of black at the upper corner of the highlight which seems like a pit in the middle of the glazes. That is a potentially tragic method of giving forms to the eye. Titian might have employed it at any time for another fifty years. The entire painting is the work of the master."

"What becomes of the Giorgionesque?"

"What indeed?" said M. de Chenonceaux. "I intend to demand a reattribution of the work, credited to you. It will be as celebrated as the reattribution of the D'Orsay desk in Manchester Square."

"You are too good."

"I am never good or kind in the practice of my profession," said the eminent scholar, "I am only accurate."

So the *Fête Champêtre* in the course of the passage of time would be removed from the small list of pictures, now no more than nine, which could be unhesitatingly ascribed to the mysterious man from Castelfranco. This provided Neil with two novel bits of information which would help modify the accepted view of the history of art: the attribution of a famous painting; the recognition that it was Titianesque, not Giorgionesque. Even the Dresden *Venus* might now with accuracy be ascribed in every detail to Titian. The rendering of the three trees in the centre and to the right of the background, and the architectural forms at the extreme right, were certainly his work. Now it seemed that a solid parallel might be effected between the treatment of the nymph in the *Fête Champêtre* and the extraordinarily warm mellifluous expressive forms of the body of the reclining goddess of Dresden. This would allow the painting – one of the most influential in history – to be given wholly to the many-sided genius of a single man.

This would be to remodel our ideas of a great artist's attainments, much as though we were to discover that Shakespeare had written the *Faerie Queene* or, as if the whole world were to become intimately familiar with all of Haydn's symphonies instead of twelve of them. On this new view, Titian is now seen to be a master of infinite variety whose art encompasses the sweetness, the delicacy, the airiness, and subtle expressionism which ordinary criticism has sometimes denied him, especially in the matter of the modelling of the naked female human form divine.

The train gave a shudder and last lurch and began to move out along the causeway and across the lagoon towards the vast railway station. A kilometre. Another. The train slowed to a crawl and proceeded gingerly through a maze of switches and sidings into the concourse where at last Neil could rise, stretch his cramped limbs, and look around for his sole piece of luggage, a narrow plastic affair crammed with writing paper and extra pairs of socks. Long acquaintance with airlines' handling of luggage had convinced him of the veteran traveller's leading principle: If you don't let them handle it, they can't lose it.

He carried a single bag, bought anything extra he required on the spot, then threw it away at departure time. Neil had deposited superfluous bits of clothing in wastepaper baskets and rubbish disposal containers in most northern European cities. He used to rent a typewriter immediately upon arrival in any given place. Once on a flight from Toronto to Regina he had observed pityingly the reactions of a fellow passenger who, upon arrival in the Regina terminal, had discovered that her cherished Russian wolfhound had been carried to Vancouver instead of being off-loaded at the same time as its mistress.

The woman had been utterly bereft, inconsolable. Her carefully poised personality had simply dissolved. Her eye makeup ran. Her enamelled cheeks cracked and crumpled. Wracked with grief, she had refused to quit the terminal building, had remained in place almost forty-eight hours refusing to be comforted until the animal was escorted eastwards to Regina and reunited with her. The reunion had been an affecting one. Photographs had appeared in the local newspaper and one of the most touching had gone out over the national wire service.

Since then Neil had refused to part with his bag. He toted a camera around his neck, a calculator in one pocket, an electric shaver in another, plenty of the local currency in a place inaccessible to any pickpocket unless his victim slept. In view of the peculiar shortage of small change usual in Italy, Neil made it a habit to collect whatever coins came his way, stockpiling them in one particular jacket pocket against the frequent necessity to dispense small gratuities or to defray other minor expenses. Whoever adjusted Venetian tariffs had carefully observed the order of impulses of the arriving travellers: First some moments passed in a lavatory, then a little time to move around and stretch, flex the muscles of the knees, then make sure one's hand luggage had not been interfered with at any point. Everything was there, the notes, the photographs, the alternate pair of thick-soled waterproof leather walking shoes. Contrary to widespread misconception, Venice, with its miles of *calle e campi*, alleys and squares, is an absolutely wonderful city in which to walk.

But in order to walk in Venice it is obligatory to ignore the inevitable Venetian advice to wanderers, *sempre diritto*. You can't proceed straight ahead in Venice, in any of the *sestieri*, for more than a few hundred yards without falling into one of the canals, or crossing a bridge, or becoming disoriented or hopelessly lost. And it does not do to study maps of the terrain – the best of maps will confuse you and may lead you into locations where you will not want to remain because they are forbidden by military or naval authorities, because they are utterly unfamiliar to yourself and *all* your guidebooks, because they smell too strongly of drains, or simply because they are blankly foreign and uninteresting.

No, in order to walk in Venice you must first spend some time in the small invaluable craft of the ACNIL, the vaporetti, and also in what are really the essential Venetian boats, the traghetti, the elegant little two-man gondolas which ferry passengers across the Grand Canal for a very modest fare at any of the two dozen stations along the way. Or you may go so far as to travel in a gondola, the uniquely Venetian water taxi. Jan Morris claims that in the modern world, "the word has only three applications: to a kind of American railway-wagon; to the under-slung cabin of an airship; to the town carriage of the Venetians." In this, as in nothing else concerning the Serenissima, the great – and indeed unrivalled – student of Venice is wrong. There is a fourth meaning of the word *gondola,* as all Canadians of a certain age will remember. That high quavering voice, that intense excitement of the invisible sporting contest observed from a vantage point "high in the gondola atop Maple Leaf Gardens." Foster Hewitt on Hockey Night in Canada.

Neil stood for a moment wondering as he had many times before who had chosen the word *gondola* so special and so closely linked to this marvellous place, to describe the broadcasting booth used in the observation of hockey games. There seemed no imaginable connection, neither in form, shape, atmosphere, or evocation of pleasure. The broadcasting *gondola* in Maple Leaf Gardens looked directly down (*sempre diritto*) from a vertiginous height upon a sheet of bluish-white ice. Nothing Venetian about that. Whoever chose the term – Foster Hewitt himself? – had plainly yearned for the delights of Venice, even Venice in winter. Were connections between Venice and Toronto – lagoons, gondolas – more multiple than they seemed?

He moved on, a little unwillingly, and cast about in his mind for elements of his halting Venetian argot. Directions would have to be given, he decided, in his usual stammering monosyllables which included neither syntax nor correct personal pronouns. He emerged onto the broad open space before and below the station to stand for a moment taking in the appearance of the Grand Canal in winter, inky and rather menacing in this light at this time of the afternoon. Light snow had fallen earlier in the day, not a rarity in a Venetian January. Now it was melting and running away in tricklings towards the landing stages and the *rio*. The squelching underfoot seemed almost excessively familiar. He looked towards the landing stages as the twilight thickened and the marvellous purple of a winter evening began to spread itself across distant terra-cotta roofs and a myriad of television aerials. There were one or two gondolas at the stages although travel by gondola is uncharacteristic of the winter months. He hefted his bag and moved tiredly down the slope, nodding towards the nearest of the gondoliers, who gave him an expressive half-bow as he approached.

"*Rio Nuovo,*" gasped Neil, and the boatman grinned as if to say, "Teach your grandmother!"

"*Al campo Santa Margherita.*"

His legs were stiff after the long train ride and he had a little difficulty stepping down into the boat which rocked slightly and gave under his feet as it took his weight. The genial boatman smiled and nodded and encouraged. It was always tricky boarding a gondola for the first time in a year or two. He set his bag down in front of him and they were off, swinging out widely into the canal – *stali, stali* – and off towards the turn into the Rio Nuovo. From here to the landing stairs near the Campo Santa Margherita it's a journey of a few hundred yards as a sensible crow would fly, but the crows don't fly in Venice, they travel by boat. The gondola ride might be twice that distance, possibly a kilometre, certainly less than a mile.

Even the short distance of a kilometre can't be traversed along the canals in winter twilight at any very great speed. The air was chilly, dank rather than cold; it might be a few degrees above freezing, not much colder than early mornings and late afternoons spent on Ontario lakes in late fall. The canal was very still;

27

little marine traffic supervened as the gondolier cried out, *"oi, oi, premi,"* swinging his craft around into the *Rio Nuovo*. The water-way narrowed slightly then grew more constricted; the gondola slid noiselessly under a bridge, the mass of the church of Saint Nicholas of Tolentino showing briefly on the left. There seemed to be a TV aerial projecting from the roof of the church of good Saint Nicholas, a curious sight, new since Neil's last visit to the district. A lurch to port in the gathering dark. It was growing ever more chill and damp. Neil gathered the robes which lay on the thwart around his shoulders. He did not want to conclude his journey with a bout of fever and chills, common enough among recent arrivals in this place. Another bridge, another church close by just to the north, this one the church of the great San Panta-leone. Before shooting the bridge, however, the gondolier slowed his boat and eased her inwards to a landing stage across the canal from San Pantaleone. A few hundred yards ahead loomed the squared shape of the municipal fire station and, facing the fire station across the *rio*, the Ca' Foscari, palace of perhaps the greatest of Venetian dynasties, legendary in its splendour and uncertain luck, celebrated in Byron's hectic tragedy.

Paying the fare and a liberal gratuity in paper money eased Neil's apprehensions about his tiny hoard of coins. He jingled his small change happily and stepped onto the landing stage with care, taking his luggage from the gondolier as he passed. It was now perfectly dark.

"Buona sera, signor."

"Grazie tante."

There came a deep soft rushing swoosh and the long black pod-shaped hull merged with the colour of the water. A creaking oar, a snatch of song from the gondolier. Then the boat vanished, turning into the Grand Canal, doubtless making for the Accademia bridge.

Saints preserve us, thought Neil, I'm back home. I'm here. San Pantaleone, feast day July 27th, Eastern martyr of the fourth century, venerated as an all-compassionate miracle worker, patron against consumption. San Nicolo da Tolentino, Augustinian, born in Tolentino 1240, died 1306, of austere and blameless life, preached daily, was most successful in bringing sinners back to the Faith, particularly famed as a miracle worker.

Miracle workers: That's what I need. I'm in the right *sestiere*. San Pantaleone, San Nicolo, and above all Santa Margherita, lend me your ears, your voices.

Darkness didn't bother Neil Tarrant, for he was now in just about the most perfect place, he thought, on the face of the earth, a few steps to northwards of the Campo Santa Margherita and his favourite resting place, the *Pensione Due Foscari,* the tiny dark constricted personal paradise which he had found for himself between the café beside the canal and the strange church / cinema which used to be dedicated to Santa Margherita and is now sacred to the luminaries of the silver screen, a peculiarly Venetian transformation. The church was closed and de-sanctified as long ago as 1810; then after the lapse of more than a century the building re-emerged into history as the place of worship of a new pantheon; it has continued thus to the present day. The ghostly presence of Santa Margherita still hovers over the *campo* which bears her name and a more real presence, the statue of the saint herself, embodies her ghostly reality atop one of the houses at the north end of the square, a few steps from Neil's *pensione completa*. Saint Margaret stands solidly and securely on top of a writhing dragon, the devil in disguise, in fact, who once upon a time swallowed Saint Margaret whole and entire.

That was a devilish tactical error for presently the wicked dragon swelled up and burst into a thousand pieces. He ought to have known better; the saint emerged smiling and unhurt from the tattered bits of dragon to bless the Campo Santa Margherita with a millennium's worth of intercession and more to come.

Before he presented himself at the Pensione Foscari Neil went round into the campo to look up at the statue of the saint, to bless himself, and to thank her for bringing him back in safety to her square where so many of his researches had begun. On the other side of the square stands the slender carmine-tinted campanile of the Carmini church sacred to Our Lady, Santa Maria del

Carmelo, with the illuminated Madonna at its top, a grateful gleam of colour and light in the January chill. I'm safe between Our Lady and Saint Margaret, thought Neil. He was certainly on the right track. He would begin again in the Carmini church, proceed from there to the Scuola di Carmini, if only for the sake of Tiepolo, then follow his over-stimulated nose. He inhaled deeply. Cookery. Later he would dine at his pensione; for the present he was content to stand at the centre of the campo and inhale the odours which drifted to him from the four nearby cafés: scampi, eel, perhaps squid, tunny, various cuts of veal, likely to be stringy but vigorously flavoured and exotically spiced. His nostrils quivered. He considered coffee. No, he decided, not just now. If he went the coffee route before dining he would arrive at his pensione shaking with nervous excitement, with a noisily protesting stomach and the beginnings of a headache. He switched his bag from his left hand to his right and strolled back to the north end of the square and down the dim alley which led to his pensione and the Rio Nuovo.

They made too much of him. They celebrated his arrival. *Il gran'signor Neiltarranti.* Neither the elderly proprietor, Signor Guicciardi, nor his second wife, the very much younger Signora Guicciardi, had ever understood that *Neil* was his Christian name, *Tarrant* his surname. He had been Signor Neiltarranti from the beginning and was fated to remain so, a circumstance which didn't disoblige him. It seemed to lend a touch of the Venetian, the eastern and exotic, to his clean-cut Canadian northerliness. Neil considered that the praiseworthy characteristics of his native land and people, immensely valuable and never to be gainsaid, yet required something of the mysterious east, some wash of antiquity cast over them in order to soften and blend in their stern outlines. All his life he had thought the Canadian in Venice the most blessed of individuals. He didn't contemplate expatriation in perpetuity, nothing of the sort. He hoped for a term of residence – in this event perhaps eight months – and other later terms of greater or lesser length in which to mollify his Canadian soul with the gleam, the terra-cottas and purples and pinks and pale off-whites and the golds of this extraordinary port.

On the morning of the following day, the last day of January, he was shown full and clear what an adoptive citizen such as himself might hope to find in the city as the beginning of a new life, for there was in the adjacent campo "all that life can provide" as there is in London. The old neighbourhood, thought Neil, as he sauntered up from his pensione towards the modest open space described in the best book about Venice as "pleasantly easygoing," exactly the right tone for the first leisurely day of an extended, perhaps somewhat laborious stay. Pleasantly – elegantly – easygoing the Campo Santa Margherita certainly is, without the prospect of water associated in most peoples' minds with the city. The campi are rarely in sight of water; this is their whole point. They are dry, rather stony, hard little city squares, the haunts of folk who really live and work here. One finds, for example, at one corner of the Campo Santa Margherita a superbly stocked *cartoleria* which was the first cause of Neil's attachment to the sestiere. The shop was a service depôt for all sorts of office machinery manufactured by Olivetti and its subsidiaries, more especially a source for typewriter rental and service. Neil used to go into the shop as soon as he arrived on any given visit to purchase a supply of typewriter ribbons, carbon paper, various pencils, some drawing equipment. He would arrange to rent a medium-sized portable typewriter. Latterly he had found himself noticing that the shop also sold, leased and serviced word-processing equipment. So far his memory had refused to retain the Venetian expression for word-processor. Later this morning he would pay a visit to the stationer's. For the moment he was happy to lounge in the window seat of the smallest of the four cafés which give on the square, to gaze across at the narrow windows of the *cambio* which he would have to visit later in the day. In Venice, he realised, the sense of neighbourhood is much stronger than in even the older parts of North-American cities. Here were a post office, a tobacconist, a daily fish and vegetable market. There seemed no need beyond the ordinary impulses of the heart ever to stir out of the campo.

All the same the campanile of the Carmini church beckoned insistently to him, could not be ignored for more than an hour.

He crumbled an iced cake, now a little stale, between his fingers, let his coffee cool without measuring its strength. No insistent waiter harried him; the city was at its emptiest although another few weeks would plunge it into pre-Lenten merrymaking. A tall elderly man in an ill-fitting two-piece suit passed the café in front of him, jacket open and flapping in a brisk breeze, his dark red shirt and suspenders hanging loosely on his meagre frame, to bring up with a sudden halt in front of a booth offering the early morning's catch of fish for sale. The man stopped abruptly like a keen kingfisher and seized a slippery denizen of the deep by the tail, hoisted it aloft and waved it about like some silvery gonfalon. He began to chatter with a stout woman of middle age with a vast spread of apron across her abdomen. An intensely expressive pantomime ensued. The fish was cast down behind the counter of the stall. The purchaser stood, arms akimbo, expressing dismay at such prices, such mercantile folly. The whole course of the debate was instantly understandable from the gestural display which punctuated it. At last the fish, or some fish, was bundled quickly into a torn sheet of villainously purple wrapping paper. Money changed hands. The buyer strode away across the campo with his fish, its scaly tail protruding under a clenched elbow. The sight of this encounter seemed to Neil to typify life in Venice: vivid, daily, unselfconscious, purposeful, fiercely comic. They were in the Dorsoduro, he remembered, the sestiere whose name he always translated for himself as "hard-shelled." The people were hard-shelled enough, living out their lives hidden from casual touristical inspection.

He had come, he saw, to the one place, the special place in all the world which he felt to define himself more perfectly than any other, where he felt – not so much perfectly at home – as perfectly able to do just what he was fitted for. It was as if in this smallish, stony, rather chilly, private assemblage of stationers and pharmacists and woollen shops and cafés and news vendors, some collection of attitudes and motives was drawn together which suited his soul more than any other.

He put his elbow on the table beside him and rested his chin on his upraised right fist in a characteristic posture. Across the campo, inescapable, pressing, stood the church of the Carmini calling to him inescapably, insinuating the trace, and more than the trace, of an idea. For there was in the Carmini the *Saint Nicholas of Bari* of Lorenzo Lotto, said by many to be the painter's nearest approach to the manner of Titian, the fruit of Lorenzo's return to Venice after many years of a provincial quasi-exile. Born about the same year as the supposed Giorgione, Neil thought, somewhere about the year 1480, give or take a few months. Left Venice (driven away?) sometime in the first decade of the new age. Most likely a native of the city. Birthplace for long disputed but now definitely supposed to have seen the light of day not far from where Neil sat on this illuminated morning. Overshadowed by more insistently celebrated contemporaries. Lorenzo Lotto seems to have been driven into departure from his native place by the sudden ascendancy of the young Titian, perhaps too of the young man from Castelfranco.

You could write a tale, Neil decided as he pondered the signal emanating from the nearby campanile, which would show Lotto, in all conscience a mysterious enough figure, as an involuntary exile forced to wander forth from his native place, somewhat like Sebastiano del Piombo, because of the magical supremacy of an unlooked-for new style, a kind of myth or dream of a new age. The sliding, acutely expressive, musical modelling of form of the Giorgionesque, the exquisite Venus, the magnificent nymph, the springtime light, the powerful delicacy of colour values – all these gracious elements of the new age seem to have impelled other mysterious ghosts to melt away until the rays of the rising sun, when once fully above the horizon, might lose their astonishing vivacity and brilliance, and settle into the assured and familiar splendour of a master's middle years. Lorenzo Lotto was able to return to Venice by 1525; he promptly executed the *Saint Nicholas of Bari*, his most Titianesque work.

Neil brushed the crumbling fragments of cake from his fingertips and looked around for someone to whom he might offer payment. Time to begin, he acknowledged to himself. He settled his bill and crossed the campo to the Carmini church where he spent the remainder of the morning looking at the *Saint Nicholas* and asking himself who had driven Lotto from the garden.

three

BRILLIANT MYSTERY OF THE FLESH, what is it happens when a century turns over as in the year 1500? The softly delicately spring-like blush of tint turns in the first decade to the assured warm radiance of summer. Around the onset of the *cinquecento* the city seemed suddenly reborn in an upthrusting bursting exaltation of colour and light such as no other city – not Paris, not Rome – can show in its history. What was going on in Venice so pressing, so swelling, as to leave upon the greatest of artists the ineradicable mark of its passing? You could only guess at this. There was an answer to the conundrum, and the answer was somewhere close at hand, yet even the question had not quite clarified itself. What am I looking for?

Lorenzo, I know, didn't paint like this before he left the city. Once in exile his special talents make themselves plain to him and he comes back fired with the spirit of emulation, can paint hero-ically in the new style. The altar dedicated to Saint Nicholas of Bari stood above and before Neil. He found himself as always trapped in the contemplation of Lotto's sudden thrust into mas-tery, a new assurance that revealed itself even more in minor mat-ters, details of passage work, than in the narrative subject, the saint's legend. In the arching corona of foliage in an incidental tree, brushed in with feathery floating softness, there was clinch-ing evidence of a new apprehension of the world, a receptivity to appearance not previously delivered by this painter. We may imagine superb reds and grave autumnal browns and purples, gold and deep blue and here and there crashing contrasting yel-lows, when we focus in imagination upon the High Venetian Renaissance, the middle noon of the Titianesque. But we do not as a rule associate the range of greens and greys and pale pale blues with which foliage is usually rendered with this high noon.

We can't find anything of the pastoral mood of eighteenth-century French landscape in the splendours of Titian whose mysterious name has been conferred upon the most erotically stimulating colour found in woman's crowning glory. The "Titianesque." Who would associate that intoxicating hue with the restraint of Watteau, the hinted grey of his shadows?

There is in Lorenzo Lotto's tree precisely this mastery of the restrained, the softly hinted fragile. And there is the same subtlety in Titian's passing glances at landscape in the years following 1525. Combination of power and restraint found only in the greatest art.

Lotto couldn't have done that tree when he was twenty. His earliest work shows in its almost proverbial "strangeness" and indecision that the great event, the coming together of looming invisible presences, had not yet happened when he was still a youth, or a young man of twenty. Nothing of his work in that first magical decade realises what is coming. The commentators say, "Yes, there is a novelty which rivals that of Giorgione in Lorenzo's first statements; they must have been associates, even friends. Giorgione must have been the comrade, then the master of the young Lorenzo. It must have been the death of the cherished friend which drove him into fifteen years of exile."

But is this right? Can it be true? Was this single unknown person of all-inspiring genius the presence in the air from whom descended like angels in the firmament a generation of painters of unrivalled originality and beauty? Wasn't the word "Giorgione" a name for the heavenly providential inspiration of an historical movement, a word without concrete embodiment, the name or one of the names for the Paraclete?

Now we're getting somewhere, thought Neil, as this reflection drifted into his mind and he began to surface from his contemplation of Saint Nicholas. Maybe we're starting to put the elusive question in the right words. What is it that impels a group of gifted men, the heirs of a definite and describable artistic tradition, suddenly to deviate into a new age, a new century, a new year, a new style? No, not just a new style. Style is easy. Manner is easy. The really new is inordinately difficult. It's the hardest task in the whole range of human experience to create a work of art in a really new way, never mind what Huey-Jack DuBoys may say.

How did they get there, what struggle brought it about? Conventional wisdom says that Lorenzo Lotto paints grey! When you look at his work beside that of Titian or Palma Vecchio or that other mysterious personage whom we should perhaps not name, Lotto remains cool, strange, an exquisite draughtsman with an extraordinary perception of the forms of the human skull but cool, cool, a natural exile. He was never able to rest, was never a happy or contented man. A tincture of nervous constraint streaks the fine fervour of his devotion to realised detail, these muted youthful tones. About 1510 these constraints tighten upon him and he goes into exile, returning after fifteen years to paint the Carmini altarpiece before which I now stand, charmed by the rise and swell of a small hill hinted in the far background, the lifting fluttering suggestion of a lively tree.

He was an outcast by character, nature, person. By fate, then. Bergamo held him. The house of Loreto welcomed him. The strangeness and poetry of the early allegories are preserved and developed in his power to confer an unearthly penetration on his mature works. All this resolves itself into what we choose to call the oeuvre of Lorenzo Lotto, wanderer, friend of Giorgione.

What do you feel, who goes with you, when your present means will not deliver what you can imagine? Think of Lotto at thirty, perplexed, half-aware that certain hints and intimations and invisible presences insist that he move. Do it, put it out there where it can be seen. Realise it. But how, he cries to himself in anguish, what am I to do? Only tell me which road to take and I will deliver all that I can imagine, for I was made for this. Do you see that lean old fellow with the hollow cheeks, a familiar Venetian form, bald over the front of the skull, doubtless often hungry, sometimes a beggar? Carries a fish under an arm. Undeniably a saint's head. Observe the purplish cast of the shadow below the left ear just where the upper and lower jaws meet. The wiry curl of the little remaining hair, something in the flush of the winypocked cheek, insignia of mortality. All this goes into a Ber-gamesque altarpiece some few years afterwards, all but the fish which has no place in that legend. Then the same skull, the identical nose and chin, reveal themselves a second time twenty years later in the portrayal of Giovanni della Volta with his wife and children, which hangs in the National Gallery. Poor Giovanni is a worried family man of middle age. His wife seems much younger than he, the children scarcely more than babies; behind the family there shines an oddly illuminated landscape with another of Lotto's enigmatic trees: the Giorgionesque brought up to date in the 1540s, when Lorenzo has learned the way to realise what he has always been able to imagine.

And what about the plumber, Sebastiano Luciani, called "the Venetian?" What kick in the backside propelled him away from Venice about 1510? Why do these distinguished exiles suddenly feel the impulse to roam just when the field had been left to them, with Giorgione dead before thirty, his greatest work still before him, the succession open?

When Neil was very young and naïve, somebody once told him (meaning to tease an innocent boy) that Sebastiano, in the course of his career as an artist in the service of the Vatican, had been honoured with the title of Papal plumber and charged with the task of maintaining the ancient leaded sewage passages of the Holy Father's apartments.

Neil had believed this for years. "Del Piombo," what an appointment for one of the greatest of these Venetian exiles, another fictitious and misleading surname and something of a joke. Oh, thou man of lead, Sebastiano! For there was certainly in this artist's work in Rome a decided heaviness, a leaden quality not found in the productions of his youth. What boy, in early days, the Venetian world displayed before him – what ambitious young painter would treat the city of the lagoons with the architectural solidity of Sebastiano's later manner?

In his early twenties Sebastiano painted like an angel. Appointed to ornament the organ shutters of the church of San Bartolommeo, when he was eighteen or nineteen, in his first important commission, what does he accomplish? There doesn't seem to be any way to explain where he found the ideas for this series of panels. His rendering of Saint Louis of Toulouse (not a great saint, not a doctor of the church nor one of the great martyrs, but still a holy man and a bishop) leaps forward immediately towards a method of delivering solid form merged in light and shadow unknown, for example, to Giovanni Bellini. The body of the saint and the richly ornate episcopal robe in which he is clad seem to curve and roll out of the surface of the picture towards us. The gold threads of the embroidery at the shoulder and collar of cope and stole, the emblems of the Sacred Heart, the flowers given in remarkable soft light, all the apparatus of episcopal authority, mitre, crozier, missal, are defined in a deeply shadowed ground which occupies the left side of the picture. The figure is ostensibly still yet seems to be pivoting with the right shoulder lowered, as if the saint were about to step down from his position and approach us, doubtless with some paternal gesture of spiritual authority.

The embroidered cope seizes and holds the viewer's attention in precisely the same manner as the puffed up blue sleeve in Titian's exactly contemporary portrait of an unknown man, for a long time thought to be Ariosto, which is in London. In both pictures a treatment of fabric suggestive of much more recent painterly methods dominates the eye of the beholder and beguiles him into keen new perceptions of the psychology of the subject of the work.

Sebastiano's modelling of the head of the saint, the hair and upper forehead mostly concealed by the heavy mitre, achieves an astonishing triumph of formal evocation by means not those of the draughtsman. The features have been touched in lightly line by line, but the element of pure drawing gives way in the finished work to a merging of outline into atmosphere suggested by the lighting of the work. A beam of light appears to fall across the tall mitre, the back of the head and the left shoulder, sharply contrasting with the darkness of the rest of the space.

The face is fully lit against a deep shade immediately next to it on the left side of the picture. The firm bony skull, the handsome straight nose, the strong and slightly protruding chin, are realised in the subtle lighting of this passage. The face seems to be illuminated in a glow emanating from another world. There is a kind of melting and dissolving action which tones down the solidity of bone, the flesh of skin and brow and lips, which achieves an effect of fusion of body and atmosphere admirably evocative of the saint's holiness and his physical good looks and impressive presence too. The work is an unlooked-for triumph, quite worthy of study beside the accomplishments of his contemporaries. The Saint Louis panel was painted at the same moment as the frescoes in the Fondaco dei Tedeschi; there are important connections of style and manner between these works, and the commentators (though not Neil Tarrant) examine the Saint Louis panel and exclaim, "Aha, the Giorgionesque!" "School of." Damning terms.

But the painting wasn't "school of" anybody Neil decided when he visited San Bartolommeo some little while after his arrival in the city. He thought of that old fraud Berenson as he drew this conclusion, remembering the invention of the phrase "amico di Sandro," and the readiness of victims to return to Boston exclaiming that they had acquired a genuine Amico.

I wouldn't even stiff Huey-Jack DuBoys with a painting by Amico di Sandro, Neil vowed. This was conceding much, for the irrepressible DuBoys had been much in his mind, even in some of his dreams lately. Somebody might sometime sell Huey-Jack a fake – a dangerous thing to do – but it wouldn't be Neil, and it wouldn't be a fake Giorgione, there being none to be had. The fake story of Sebastiano, the so-called Papal plumber, had coloured Neil's youth but had not led him into the paths of deceit. Sebastiano had in fact left Venice at about twenty-five, but not because he wanted to become a plumber.

Probably too many people had told him that he was painting in a strange new style like certain other disobedient young men. Why couldn't they behave? They were all the same, these youngsters, an ill-mannered set of turbulent boys who ought to cleave to the methods of their admired elders and give up this effeminate cloudy mysterious softness. Neil could imagine an artist's response to this counsel: Silence, exile, and cunning. Exile first of all. He went to Rome and became in due course not the Papal plumber but the master of the Papal seals and sealed official documents, these confidential papers invariably being closed up by huge seals of pure lead, each one ornamented by a relief designed by the official painter-sealer, in this event the great Sebastian. The sobriquet "del Piombo" meant nothing more than that the painter – by then an exceedingly well-conducted friar – had achieved a dignified and useful position at the papal court. Master of the Seals. Some such title would very well describe the mature Sebastiano whose work became increasingly solid, even heavy, in the end closely united to architectural form and rendering.

There could be no more pathetic reversal of inclination than that of poor Sebastiano Luciani, enmeshed in the labyrinth of Vatican policy, attempting a fusion of artistic conceptions which was deeply against nature, the wedding of the Giorgionesque and the style of Michelangelo. No effort of spiritual contortion could have imprisoned the primaveral spirit of Venice in 1510 in the heavily architectural and sculptural conceptions of the Michelangelesque. As well marry Venus and Mars.

Sebastiano del Piombo may fail as an artist but he fails greatly. In the beginning he had the same illimitable endowment as Lorenzo Lotto, Palma, the boy Titian. Just before he left Venice Sebastiano achieved a masterpiece in a purely Venetian mode which at the same time shows elements of the self-alienation in his nature which will in the end make him the friend and follower of Michelangelo. This is the painting displayed over the high altar in the church of San Giovanni Crisostomo, the fabulous *San Giovanni Crisostomo with six saints,* in which the artist's divided sensibility and impending self-exile are predicted. It is a coming-together of the Venetian and Roman impulses which lead in the end to Sebastian's appointment as *magister sigilli.* Saint John Chrysostom, "the golden-mouthed," sits in the upper centre of the picture at the focal point of the viewer's contemplation. But the great orator is not shown speaking. He is copying some sacred text into a large open missal which he holds balanced before him on a small desk.

Three exquisite female figures – young saints – stand in the lower left foreground, their heads and features given in the manner of Giovanni Bellini. Behind Saint John the columns of some grandly solid portico rise up to dominate most of the background while the figures of three male saints, old, middle-aged and young, occupy most of the right side of the picture.

Only in the upper right corner do light and sky and distance intrude. Here they are given with the characteristic impulse of the Venetian painter, whatever his age and stylistic affinities in the first decade of the *cinquecento*. Three-quarters of the available space is given to architectural form and to a quasi-architectural arrangement of the seven human figures in the picture. One apprehends vividly the impulses in Sebastiano's art which will send him away into a lifetime's inquiry into the nature of solid sculptural form, the columnar. But the sky and the light can still be seen in the work, in their fugitive position in the upper corner. The painting is almost an autobiographical presentation of the dilemma of its painter. Here is a fully realised expression of what all men of talent must have felt in that city in that decade.

If I am the man that I am, if I have these talents, but not those, can I paint as these impulses from this place dictate? It is the question that history imposes upon every artist, painter, writer, musician, architect. Some places and times impose demands so specific, so exigent, that artists whose natures do not respond to them must go elsewhere if they are to have their lives. Sebastiano Luciani, called "Veneziano," loses those names, "man of light," "Venetian," and becomes "the man of lead" who impresses papal authority upon soft dull metal.

Perfection in art demands the absolutely free unreserved wedding of talent and sensibility to whatever the moment in time exacts. You have to be completely alert, ready, flexible. You have to go where you can live and work.

Somebody had declared that a man is more like his time, his

age, his historical epoch, than he is like his brother. It is so. Lorenzo, Sebastiano, weren't brothers; they were more alike than brothers. They made more than fraternal responses to their times.

Neil began to fidget and stammer with excitement as he left San Giovanni Crisostomo. He had business at the nearby post office. There might be official communications waiting for him there. Perhaps he had spent an irresponsible amount of time – weeks and weeks – in the Carmini, San Bartolommeo, San Giovanni Crisostomo. But he didn't think so.

Neil was starting to sense in himself the approach of a qualitative leap in his ability to judge his findings. He moved in a controlled saunter towards the post office, thinking over the seven figures in that altarpiece, the three marvellously disposed figures of young and holy women, the conjunction of their heads, the relations among those heads. Then the dominant position of the central figure and the gradual movement of the eye towards the right of the work where the head of the middle-aged male saint is poised just at the edge of the space. There was something special about that head, balding, bearded, strong nose, a piercing left eye clearly visible, power in the head and the wide, unexpectedly sensual mouth. It was the head of Huey-Jack DuBoys. Neil racked his brain, trying to recall which saint in the calendar was supposed to be represented by this particular figure.

There was a pulse or nerve beating slowly in his right temple, a physical phenomenon which in Neil's experience often preceded a severe bout of depression. Something was about to happen to him. That was certain. He had invariably found that the onset of a more or less deep depression always forewarned some important step forward in his thinking. Because of this pattern he welcomed, even luxuriated in bad feeling, knowing it would bring light in its train.

He was nearing some third mysterious fact in his chain of evidence. He almost had it. And here it came! No associate of the necessarily mythical man from Castelfranco could ever have conceived, much less realised, a portrayal of a head so perfectly the embodiment of all that a petroleum engineer from West Texas was. Only a *Roman* painter could have done it, or a painter about to go in that direction.

As he went up the wide steps and entered the Central Post Office Neil felt a wave of dreadful lassitude and dejection pass through him. His sight seemed to dim. It was only with difficulty that he forced himself to remain immobile in the queue in front of the *raccomandata* window. There ought to be a registered reply to an inquiry he had set on foot a week or two after his arrival in the city. He had visited the post office almost every day for more than a month in the hope of a speedy response to his requests. Then he had had to decide that repeated inquiries wouldn't contribute to a quick reply, just as a watched kettle refuses to boil.

But a day or two ago he had received at his pensione the small cardboard notification that a registered letter was waiting for him and would be surrendered to him at the post office upon presentation of adequate means of identification (passport, visa, certificate of baptism). Standing in a lineup was for Neil, especially in his present state of mind, a penance or torment which might earn him an eternal reward. The lineup shortened in front of him and he jiggled excitedly from one foot to the other, stepping heavily at one moment on the toes of an elderly signora immediately behind him. He turned around, blushing, to offer apologies, to find himself confronted by so unswerving a stare of dismissal that his muttered conventional regrets died in his dry throat. Now he was at the wicket. A sour visage behind the grille eyed him appraisingly. Stammering broken words, unnerved by the brief encounter with the stern signora, her eyes boring into his back, Neil produced his passport, added to it his notification of a registered letter, and breathed a sigh of relief as the grim postal clerk turned from the counter and disappeared into the recesses of rows and rows of pigeonholes and shelves. Clouds of dust hung over the scene. An unnaturally prolonged wait. At these times Neil invariably felt strong sensations of irrational guilt, suspicions that unnamed authorities were about to leap out at him, seize him, demand further proof of his identity and reject his Canadian passport as unacceptable. Everybody knows that you can still acquire a Canadian passport with the utmost facility, the spies' passport.

The photograph in Neil's passport was just like all such photographs, a gross caricature of his features taken in the kind of light used to take pictures of axe-murderers for circulation in public buildings. He glanced nervously around, half expecting to find his passport photo blown up to hideous proportions and hanging with those of other fugitives from justice in a prominent place not far from where he stood. Perhaps the signora behind him had picked it out. She gave him an almost imperceptible shove between the shoulder blades as the official returned to the grille holding a fat legal envelope well-wadded with documents.

At the sight of the envelope Neil's nervousness, depression, and fear of prosecution for some nameless crime vanished into the depths of his unconscious, doubtless to return at some future crisis-point. He recovered his documents and letter from the hands of the official who gave him a radiant and expressive grin as the papers passed between them. The good reputation of Venetian officialdom was at once restored in Neil's mind. He knew better than to proffer a gratuity, but he leaned forward and spoke words of heartfelt thanks, at the same time extending his hand through the narrow aperture beneath the grille.

A qualified handshake was achieved and he turned away, clutching his letter – the Castelfranco permissions – to his breast.

It had taken him about eight weeks of deliberate correspondence to reach this stage, the point at which the permissions he required would either be granted or denied. And he could tell, from long experience of European bureaucratic procedure, that an envelope of this bulk contained acceptance. Refusal would have been meagre. Acceptance meant parchment, seals, copies in triplicate, many documents, request for payment of further fees, possibly invitations to dine with this or that curator or deputy-mayor.

He strode briskly back to his campo where he intended to forego the pleasures of the pensione's set luncheon table in order to grapple with café cuisine and a better bottle of wine than usual.

For the examination of these papers he would require tranquillity and quietude, not the excited exclamations of the Guicciardi chiming in his ears. They were so good to him and so interested in all that he did that he could never quite take in any reading done in their presence. With the Signor and Signora Guicciardi the coldness of print was inadmissible. Conversation was everything. Below the Rialto bridge he hopped aboard the vaporetto for the few minutes' ride to the landing stage next to the Ca' Rezzonico where he found himself 300 metres from the Carmini. Squid, he thought, for the hell of it. He had never eaten squid but today he would attempt it. In oil and butter, and the hell with Canadian qualms.

It tasted, he concluded, like the crypto-meat in Shopsy's wieners; there was the same springy and resistant quality to the flesh as one attempted to divide it with the incisors. Then the process of chewing seemed to reduce the resistance offered to ingestion, though without quite allowing the bitten-off chunk to be shredded into small bits suitable for swallowing. It didn't so much appear that the squid was tough, or at any rate tougher than other squid. It resisted ingestion. You had to grapple with it, while the oil, butter, chopped onion, celery and some leafy green crinkled substance that might have been spinach but could have been anything, slid down the throat conferring the conviction of nutriment without its actuality. Neil may have left some squid on his plate, but he felt that he had done a noble thing in attempting the dish. He resolved to insist to the proprietors of the Nag's Head that they add the item – he would instruct them in its preparation – to their evening menu as an exotic challenge to regular diners. He would have had squid. Why shouldn't others suffer it too? Might be a big hit with the estate planners and the magazine editors.

When he opened his fat letter and separated its various communications from each other, he saw that his infinitely delicately worded applications, his fine courtesy, his lofty credentials, had done their work. Yes, he could photograph the altarpiece according to the provisions in force against the use of excessively strong

46

lighting near the work. Yes, he could once again have access to the Giorgione archives and records, as also the collection of documents and slides relating to the altarpiece. The coffers in the sacristy would be opened for him as they had been upon his previous visit. Certain new paleographic evidence was available for his attention. He need only present these official letters of attestation (*letteri di attestazione*) in order to commence his inquiries which, the civic authorities hoped and trusted, would be crowned with the richest success.

Get thee to Castelfranco, he thought, noticing as he did so that he had spilt his wine all over the letter with the biggest red seals on it. Maybe nobody would notice or care.

four

AS WITH MOST JOURNEYS UNDERTAKEN IN THIS LIFE, there are two ways to go from Venice to Castelfranco, the long and the short. On that windy March morning Neil chose to take the long way around, proceeding across the causeway by motorbus to the mainland and from there north to Treviso where a somewhat inconvenient journey might be interrupted for morning coffee. In Treviso towards ten in the morning, our poor sensitive pilgrim felt a vague queasiness induced by the motion of the antique vehicle in which he rode. There were stops at every wayside crossing, and though the terrain is flat and the distance to Treviso not more than twenty miles, the ride discomforted the investigator. He felt overblown, inflated from within by possibility.

Neil was never an ambitious man. He had not undertaken the study of these works of art in the cheap spirit of revisionism. He had no wish to undermine reputations or to baffle and inflame older and more celebrated scholars. He thought that he had hold of a truth which when communicated to the scholarly community would spread its influence in wider and wider circles so that in the end the High Renaissance would be visible in a different light. It would seem to be even more self-assured, more heroic in manner and gesture, readier to leap ahead to formidable new solutions to ancient problems: The problem of the depiction of light and shadow; the problem of the right method of rendering the tone of naked human flesh; the problem of the relation of this world to the next in strictly pictorial terms, a conundrum solved much earlier for literature by a Florentine. Coming at Castelfranco, putative birthplace of the sanctified mythical figure whom he had expected to send into exile forever from the world of the historic, the true inhabitants of past time, was to the investigator like forcing a breach in the walls of a storied fortress, the towers and battlements of a stately name. There might be an impiety implied.

Half-an-hour spent on a breezy terrace in front of the best café in Treviso, wind curling under the skirts of his coat, tugging at sleeves and buttons, dispelled queasiness but brought other discomforts. Was the next bus, due at 11:00 AM, truly an express to Castelfranco? Would there be further swayings and saggings on worn springs, smells of questionable fish and cheese in the packed interior? Excitement was making him nauseous. There might be something to be said for hiking the remaining distance, but unfortunately it was a distance outside the ordinary range of the hiker, about sixteen miles. What about a hired car? This seemed a fruitful conception and a brief search located a driver and car. Negotiations over fare and gratuity proved conclusive; towards 11:00 Neil found himself bowling along the wide flat highway which connects these points. Here the Veneto remains level but there are already in the distance to the northwest the shadowy forms of sizeable hills which are only the foothills of a great mountain range with heights and crossings unimaginable from the lowland.

Neil had told his driver to set him down within easy walking distance of the storied little town, so that he could approach it on foot as a pilgrim should. Besides he needed a walk. And as the long undulating line of hilly shadows clarified itself in the mid-morning light, and the breeze sang in the windows of the smart Fiat sedan which bore him briskly towards his destiny, his heart lifted and he knew himself to be on the threshold of a final entry-way to the truth. He felt as if he were actively participating in the reconstruction of a crime during the final chapter of some masterwork of detective fiction. They passed swiftly through the tiny settlement of some hundred souls where George had been born not far from the point at which Neil intended to quit the car. It came to a stop and he got out. Money changed hands. The driver, a certain Agostino Trevisano, swung his shining sedan around

49

and headed back down the highway. Neil squared his shoulders. With a walk of some mile-and-a-half before him, time just coming up to noon, he prepared to advance upon the walls, the towers, the absurd little moat, of the old fortified cathedral town in which he was to confront fate.

Standing alone in the roadway, no traffic in sight, only the sound of a rising wind whispering in his ears, farm workers doubtless relaxing over their noon wine in the outbuildings which stood to left and right of the road at a little distance, he gazed towards Castelfranco, "the castle of the Franks," (Another link with Toronto, equally storied city with its own Castle Frank.) and began to place one foot in front of the other. The silhouette of the place started to detach itself in realised perspective from the dim shadows on the uplands beyond. It was just such a townscape as might have been viewed five hundred years before by the children who became Lorenzo, Palma, Tiziano, Sebastiano, the country of the Veneto gleaming with its never-to-be-found-elsewhere radiance. Stepping into the painting. I've been framed, he thought, advancing.

Crenellations, battlements, why? The town still retained some traces of its mediaeval state, a posture of defence, protective circlet of water, gates. A cathedral town too, dignity seemingly quite out of proportion to the size of the community within the walls. Surprisingly a hillside town, set on the first of the rising levels of ground which roll away to the northwest. Neil could feel the tugging in his calves and thighs which signalled a slow ascent, even though the landscape seemed unaltered and the horizons as distant as ever. A few steps more and he was at the gate, within the gate, not far from the Cathedral of San Liberale.

He found within the enclosure the cold wind of March baffled and turned off by the walls and the crouching buildings. The Palazzo Costanza, small, colourful, much in need of repair, beyond that the chancery office of the diocese where he was to present his letters of accreditation.

An hour's inquiry located Monsignor Ildebrando Antoniutti, empurpled as to sash and prelatical cloak, in fact a domestic prelate and the chief diocesan official under the bishop. In local influence Monsignor Antoniutti might even be said to weigh heavier in any imaginable scale than His Grace himself, for the bishop was now old and sick and approaching the age of mandatory retirement. There seemed small doubt that the good monsignor would succeed his father in God at some time not far distant. In the meantime he occupied himself with study, with the administration of the diocese and with his extraordinary knowledge of the works of art and the antiquities of the cathedral city. He was not a native of the place but of Bergamo, sometimes felt himself resented by the people of Castelfranco as an intruder, may perhaps have assisted Neil's researches in unconscious response to the suspicion.

The monsignor seemed almost elated, certainly enthusiastic, as he examined Neil's letters, seals, identifying documents. He held a page of one of the letters to the light, then held it briefly to his nose. "Not blood," said the monsignor.

"An indifferent local wine," said Neil smiling. The monsignor chuckled.

"First to the altar, then to the sacristy," he said. He enfolded Neil in a near embrace and together they paced out of the chancery offices, secretaries and commissioners exchanging puzzled looks behind them. Not in living memory had the monsignor seemed so cordial, so receptive to foreign inquiry. What could lie behind his open and forthcoming manner to this young scholar who seemed unimportant enough in appearance, not at all the sort of young man (Alexander, Napoléon) who topples empires and causes epochs to revolve at his command. The diocesan functionaries listened in perplexity as the monsignor's voice died away in the distance.

"... such a renowned work of art as is happily ours ... glory of Castelfranco ... commanded by the most august family of the Costanza ... but you will see for yourself."

"I have been here before, Monsignor."

"Ah yes, Signor Tarrant. Who is not familiar with your little publications? I have examined them myself and I find your views in all respects convincing. Perhaps you now contemplate an extended work of scholarship on this matter?"

"That would depend on my findings, my dear Monsignor. I feel that I may be on the point of an important revelation."

They came into the cathedral together and stood in the transept on the Gospel side of the altar, gazing at the magnificent Costanza altarpiece, *The Madonna enthroned with the Infant Jesus above San Francisco and San Liberale.* Perhaps the pivotal work of the High Renaissance, certainly to be ranked with one or perhaps two of the works of Leonardo in that respect. The final imposition of the natural and the open upon the formal and the closed. What is to be said about the Castelfranco altarpiece? Shall we simply treat it as two paintings in one? An interior and two formally displayed symbolic figures of saints, monk and warrior, closed in deeply shadowed wall and supported by precise geometrical forms of marble tiling depicted in exact and highly abstract perspective. Above this, the dividing line which severs the work in almost perfect halves, with the enthroned Virgin, Holy Child at ease upon her right knee, poised in mid-air, a towered villa at some distance behind the figure of the Blessed Mother on her right. On her left a curving road emerging from a copse. In the middle distance the portico of some temple, the customary airy trees and foliage of the "Giorgionesque" and then hills, clouds, the glorious heavens.

Like pure being as such, the work is full of puzzles. What sort of room are these saints standing in? It must be a great and solid work of building, as the marble floor, the high crimson wall, the footings of the Virgin's throne all suggest. Plainly this is the interior of some house of worship. Yet above the border of the enclosing wall, which seems perhaps to be formed of wood over which crimson fabric has been applied, the formal architectural support for the heavenly virginal throne must, logically, project backwards into the space of the picture, that is, out of the enclosed interior into an illogical space where it floats according to a different mode of existence. From this seat Jesus and Mary look down upon the saintly warrior and monk with ineffable love.

The lower half of the work is executed with close, almost embroidered details of tracery, in the knight's swordbelt, in the boss of the coat of arms depicted in the lower centre of the picture, and most of all in the rendering of the cloth which drapes the Virgin's knees, a cloth figured with flowers and crowns, scrolls and what appears to be a heaped-up basket of fruit – all these figures deriving from ancient emblematic traditions. This strictly detailed embroidery of emblem is carried up into the higher reaches of the work in only one place, the painted drapery which hangs behind the head of the Virgin, marked out carefully with forms of artificial and formal leaf and flower. Around this single incursion of human art into the heavens lies the lonely breathing sky and the attenuated mists of the Veneto.

"It isn't two distinct paintings," said Neil in an undertone, "it's unquestionably the work of a single person, but a person of two minds."

"Exactly what I think myself," said Monsignor Antoniutti.

Together they moved closer and studied the picture from every possible angle.

"The lower half might be by Bellini."

"But it isn't. We know that. We have the documents."

"What I meant was that the intelligence that originally conceived the work was employing something of the manner of the later Bellini, perhaps in youth, in the earliest exercise of its strength. It may be the termination of an apprenticeship. Then the skies open and this intelligence sees in a new way. The walls and the roof open and there are the Madonna and Child. Two minds, one man."

"I will take you to the room of the coffers," said the monsignor, "I have everything waiting that is necessary. I have had the enlargements made which you requested. The correspondence is there for inspection, lying in the coffers where you first discovered it three years since."

In the recesses of a kind of muniment room or records office, some six hundred years old and filled with the atmosphere of ancient times, dust, candle smoke, incense, indifferently washed human bodies, decaying wood and paper, there lay five enormous black wooden chests. The smallest of these coffers is much larger and deeper than a modern steamer trunk, with a lid so heavy that, falling, it might crush anything caught between it and the sill of the chest. One or two of the chests are more than five feet deep. All are crammed, packed, with the official documents of the diocese and its cathedral church, accumulated over centuries.

It was in the largest and deepest and perhaps the oldest of these antique coffers that Neil had discovered, during the course of his first visit to the cathedral nearly three years before, the deeply browned, curled, almost unopenable parchments which contained the correspondence of the Costanza family with the bishop of the day ordering the execution of the altarpiece now, five centuries later, a central problem for art historians. The Costanza correspondence in several places named, or could certainly be argued to have named, the artist chosen for the commission. These letters remained where Neil had discovered them.

"Nothing has been moved; they are in the fourth coffer," said the monsignor. Neil started to count down through the masses of crumbling documents until he came to the stratum where the Costanza materials were deposited, carefully wrapped at some primordial time in lengths of fine leather from which still rose the faint smell of animal matter.

"When I came here three years ago," said Neil, "I was the first person to unwrap these letters since they were written and received 500 years ago." He went to his knees. To his surprise the monsignor knelt humbly beside him. It was a great moment, a short time of instantaneous revelation. Neil unfolded the leather with minute caution. Too rough handling might reduce it to dust, the folds and seams being cracked with age. The dozen or so parchment leaves which lay within were in an extraordinary state of preservation, but they too might only be handled with the extremest care. The two men stood up and the monsignor stripped away the unfolding leather while Neil held the precious communications by their edges, handling them as one might an infant child, with radical tenderness and attention.

They laid the letters on top of the adjoining coffer.

"These are the ones, the letters which commissioned the altar-piece, propose payment, suggest various legendary subjects, give instruction as to colour and method of siting the piece. It's all here. The addressee is sometimes the diocesan official charged with the maintenance of the cathedral, sometimes the chief crafts-man of the maintenance staff, a carpenter and a glassmaker. Four of the letters are directed to the painter himself, by name, that is, by his sobriquet or cognomen in the argot of the Veneto. It is these four letters which will resolve the question, which must be photocopied with the greatest care, and the photocopies enlarged so as to show the writing and the name or names of the artist. He seems to have one single sobriquet which can be spelled in any of several ways."

"Still a common practice of the district," said Monsignor Antoniutti. "Among the younger clergy of the *capitulum* I am known as Brando! Also as Tonio. Sometimes as TonTon. At other times the names are rather less reverent, as when disciplin-ary measures are at issue."

"Inescapable and truly of the Veneto," said Neil. "In the Anglo-Saxon world these nicknames might be less multiple. I have no nickname. There isn't much you can do with *Neil*. Some-times I wish I were a less serious fellow; then I might have an affectionate nickname. Our painter certainly had at least three."

"The legendary Giorgione is said to have been called Zozo or again, Zonzon. And sometimes, most affectionate of all, Zor-zone, with the initial consonant produced by the tip of the tongue and upper incisors, *ts, ts, ts*. As 'Tsortsone.'"

"Quite right, and none of these formations is found in the letters, not once. Here, let's look at the key passages."

He took a magnifying lens from his pocket and handed it to the monsignor. Then he lifted the first of the four key letters care-fully from the pile and began to unfold it. There was an awed silence.

"I did this three years ago," said Neil, grimacing as he eased the folds of the precious document apart, "and I still have dreams about it. A case of fools rushing in. I hadn't the faintest notion of what I was about to find, and very little sense of the fragility of the documents." With great deliberation he continued to ease open the sheet. At length the unfolded parchment, its folds deep and almost splitting, lay to one side of the lid of the coffer.

"Now take my lens and read the passages which I point out."

He began to move his forefinger along the faded brown lines of manuscript done in the calligraphy of the end of the fifteenth century.

"Paleographer's work," muttered Monsignor Antoniutti.

"Pretty nearly," said Neil. "It's a hard hand to read but it can be done. I received my paleographic assistance from the Pontifical Institute in Toronto, where we have the best paleographers in North America."

"You have not been able to show them these letters."

"No. I had only to give the date of the correspondence and the type of parchment and the characteristics of the writing, ink, and so forth, and they were able to produce enlargements of microfilms showing an almost identical handwriting. Not the same man, but a close contemporary and neighbour. It was then that I knew what I had seen here three years ago, for we do not find in these letters in this handwriting the names 'Zozo,' 'Zonzon' or again 'Zorzone.' The vowel sound given in this writing is not a rendering of that vocalic phone. What we have here is handwriting which gives the sounds of the *ahh* or short, breathy initial vowel. Or again the *ya* sounds. These names are 'Zanzan' and 'Zanzian' and quite often 'Zianzan.' The person addressed is the young Titian. The altarpiece was commissioned from him, fact, and wholly executed by him, fact. That makes five, enough for my purposes."

Monsignor Antoniutti muttered, "You have mentioned two. Are you assured of your three other facts?"

"Perfectly."

"Show me some of the other letters. Isn't the writer Marcello Costanza?"

"He is the author; the handwriting may be that of a secretary."

"Costanza as the author, then, must have been on the closest terms of intimate friendship with the painter. He speaks very informally. He seems to treat him almost as a son."

"That is precisely my point. They were friends: they knew one another intimately for another thirty-five years, at least until the 1530s, when Marcello Costanza disappears from historical record. He appears and reappears in the public life of the Veneto and in the life of Venice for more than three decades, very often in association with Tiziano as patron, counsellor, friend. He offered employment to the painter's brother when he abandoned his own painting career. He helped Tiziano Vecelli many times with gifts of money, and helped him to get commissions from many distinguished patrons. The thing is as clear as daylight; this is the first work of Titian set on foot by Marcello Costanza and these letters are directed to the painter, whom he knew and loved, in a profusion of verifiable detail, not to a ghostly being who cannot in fact be traced to any historical location."

"You are apparently quite right in all of this," said the monsignor tranquilly. "You are going to turn our little city upside down. We will be overrun by crowds of experts, archaeologists, photographers, writers of monographs, journalists. It seems too bad."

"You will not stand in their way."

"No," said the monsignor sadly, "we will not stand in their way."

"And we can make the copies which I require? I have technical assurances that photocopying won't hurt the letters."

"All is in readiness in my offices, exactly as you requested. You will have to agree to certain stipulations."

"Certainly, assuredly. Shall we make our copies at once?"

"Just as you wish."

They gathered up the dozen letters, placing the four crucial sheets on the top of the pile, and went back to the chancery office. There they found a battery of state-of-the-art copying machines which somehow seemed too costly and too multiform for a small up-country diocese. Catching Neil's look of surprise, the monsignor smiled contentedly.

"It is a small diocese but we have many inquirers about our

works of art. And then there is the diocesan business, many out-lying parishes, many changes in the hours of Mass."

Somehow the machines didn't look like they had been arranged just to copy out the hours of Mass and Confession. They had an air of being able to produce instant publicity on the grand-est scale. Neil eyed them with obscure feelings of disquiet which were much mitigated when the monsignor, taking charge of the process himself, produced magnificent copies of all twelve letters, adjusting the controls of the copier until he was able to make reproductions which were virtually identical in every respect to the originals, except for the fact that the texture of the parchment and the faded sepia of the script were not delivered. Otherwise the writing was as sharp and clear as could be desired.

"Next year I'll be able to do them in colour," said the monsig-nor, "and then they'll almost be criminal forgeries. But these are excellent copies. You can reproduce the smallest detail of the script in any size you wish without loss of definition. The names which you have put in question, the formation of the letters and therefore the spellings, can be enlarged to the point where your findings will be beyond dispute."

"I know. I realise that," said Neil, moving uneasily from one foot to the other. It was now late in the afternoon and there were one or two formalities to be gotten through. Attestation by a high diocesan official – in the event Monsignor Antoniutti him-self – that the papers were all that they claimed to be: datings and stampings and dealings. At length the legal formalities were com-plete and the rights of all the parties fully defined and protected. Should Neil wish to publish reproductions of the letters any-where, acknowledgement of their source must be made, permis-sion to publish sought and granted, a licensing fee paid. No alter-ation of the appearance of the copies could be made, no collaging or superimposition of one image on another could be effected.

All imaginable use of the materials was described and the inter-ests of the diocese, payment of fees, reservation of residual and unstipulated rights, given under seal and guaranteed. By 5:15 Neil was free to depart, carrying a bulky sheaf of new materials wrapped in heavy clear plastic sheeting, the kind used in North America to secure construction sites in winter. He must have been toting close to a hundred largish sheets of heavy copying paper in this sizeable bundle as he trotted to the local bus station.

This time he took the shortest way back, straight down an excellent modern highway in an express bus which left Castelfranco every evening at 6:00 bound for Venice on a tight schedule. The bus was half-empty, a fact which surprised Neil. He expected to find it full of travellers from the province eager to taste the delights of the lagoons. Instead it seemed to transport tired workmen from some construction job in Castelfranco to their homes in Mestre where the bus made its only stop before crossing the causeway and entering the terminal. By this time, almost 7:30, it was plain Neil wouldn't be able to proceed to the next stage of his research – the making of many blowups – that evening. He had arranged matters with the manager of the stationery shop on the Campo Santa Margherita, where enlarging equipment could be rented by the hour or day, with trained attendants available to operate it. But no definite time had been set for the job. He had wanted to get started on it that evening if possible. There was a faint possibility that the stationer's shop might be open on a midweek night. The work would only take an hour or two to complete. If only he might have gotten there before they shut for the night. He felt himself possessed by a dreadful demon of immoderate haste for which he could give no reason. There was always tomorrow.

He desperately wanted to see those fated, expressive, essentially Venetian nicknames spelled out in large revealing writing, the declaration which all the world would come to recognise. There would be many pictures in major magazines, maybe on TV.

Art historian makes major discovery
Story of mankind revised

The vulgarity of this conception, worthy of Huey-Jack DuBoys, made Neil shiver as he stepped aboard the vaporetto for the quick passage towards the centre of the city. How could he conceive of such a shoddy reputation, how reconcile the splash in the media with his years of patient investigation? Of course they couldn't be reconciled. He felt some of the impulse to haste leave him as his landing stage came in sight, lit only by a few glinting beams from the shaded windows of casa or palazzo. It was now full night and the breeze which had persisted through the day was strengthening, curling over the roofs and along the curves of the Grand Canal. The water seemed unfamiliarly high. Was some unusual tidal drift in play? He dodged in and out of the obscure alleys which led to his campo, then debouched suddenly from a dark turning onto the modest stretch of the familiar square. The tobbaconist was still open, as were two, no three, of the cafés. The stationer's was closed for the night; nothing to be done until tomorrow morning.

All at once he realised that he was at the end of his physical resources, fatigued to the point where hunger and thirst were no longer in play. He might have a slight fever, more from excitement than anything else. He turned on his heel, shrugged his floppy bundles of papers more securely under an arm and walked slowly back to his pensione where his host and hostess made much of him, babied him a little with very hot soup and a litre of some excellent red. Kindness and hot food were too much for Neil. He began to nod off and actually had to be assisted upstairs to bed, pursued by affectionate chuckles from the two Guicciardi. He undressed automatically, fell into bed and was asleep at once.

Towards midnight the wind rose high and the sound of moving water rippled and washed through Venice. There was mist, swirling, curling in and out of ill-fitting window frames. Very late there came an explosive sound in Neil's bedroom as a violent gust snapped his windows open on their rickety hinges. All the canals of Venice began to sing to him, chanting an incomprehensible invitation. He sat up in bed and gazed in amazement at the open windows through which, he saw, a mysterious figure was advancing to salute him.

five

IT WAS STILL BLACK DARK OUTSIDE, morning some hours distant, but the advancing figure was clearly visible, framed in a gleaming illumination whose source seemed undiscoverable, neither moonlight nor starlight. Behind this illogical light, high in the sky above and across the neighbouring canal, dark grey clouds parted against a darker sky, flying past like hurrying phantoms. There was a freshening air abroad in the night which seemed to Neil to agitate the bedclothes and the curtains suspended around the open windows. He was certainly wide awake, for he could feel the breeze which cooled his cheeks, hot from several hours' burial under blankets. His face was flushed, feverish with excitement. The breeze made a hectic music in the shutters and curtains, rustled and whistled in various papers and envelopes which he'd left exposed on an escritoire. Some writings were blown to the floor but Neil made no move to recover them. It seemed wisest to remain half-reclining as this mysterious airy personage took on a definite outline.

It was the figure of a full-grown man who seemed to move with a strolling gait, his legs propelling him forward in a relaxed saunter, under a rich robe which was drawn closely around him, only the feet visible under the hem of the garment. He seemed to float rather than walk, upheld in the middle air by an invisible force, some updraft like those which support seagulls in flight for hundreds of miles. No question here of the inexplicable. Neil felt no wonderment at the sight of this figure drifting into his life from the outer night. In another setting with a charnel or infernal tone he might have experienced terror, at least bewilderment, a sense of the marvellous, but here there was only a serene assurance that the easily sauntering gentleman wouldn't ever find his poise threatened. Neil made as if to move, to sit fully erect, to gesticulate. The light around the figure intensified itself momentarily as though transmitting a message. He understood that he was to remain where he was. Perhaps the intensity and tone of the strange illumination were to serve as code or warning signal. There was a perpetual alteration in the nuances of light and shadow which played in the vibrant wash of golden glow accompanying the stranger's motion, something like the management of shadow and light in certain celebrated works of art. This observation caused Neil to imagine that rather than being immersed in an other-worldly supernatural manifestation of some disturbing kind he was being raised up into the interior structure of a great picture, as if being formed himself into an attendant personage inside the frame.

The golden light changed, enlarging its scope, spreading into the corners of the bedchamber, harvesting little pockets of shadow where walls and floors came together, as if forming the defining edges of the action now in play. It was like living or dreaming in a box of art. The corners were darkly present. There was a floor, a ceiling, but they were not figured in the design. He was aware of a perfect blend around his extremities, his feet and fingertips, of soft air neither too cool nor too warm. Often at moments of great tension or excitement Neil's limbs grew cold as if his pulse and circulation had slowed. Tonight his body seemed bathed in a sweet circumambience which felt liquid and flowing and just right, like a bath of crystal light. There was a quickening intoxication in this awareness.

Every person alive who truly rejoices in existence has known and longs to revisit certain treasured states of being, times and places and seasons which have been for him or her the ultimate times, the best times of life. A scent of hawthorn in nearby bushes, the sound of a small waterfall, a cavernous black night sky stippled with millions of bright stars, early morning sunlight on still water, in acute sensibilities combinations of statement from all the senses at once which rise into gravely heightened response, may vest the soul in the possession of wholly given, wholly stated moments of presence in which the responding sensibility becomes certain that it is no mere perceiver or witness of what is happening but a fully endowed participant in the scene. The occurrence is going on *around and behind* the fully aware spirit and there seems no bifurcation of self and other, viewer and world, in the structure of the event. You are in the scene and the scene enfolds you. You might (if you liked) put out your tongue and taste the flowing air.

Neil was now in such a state. He had first of all a premonitory conviction that something intolerably good and important was about to take place, not just for him but for everything present in the moment. He leaned forward, cautiously easing himself into the still time; as he did so the entire – the fully formed – presence gave itself to him. He had an overwhelming apprehension of the end of winter, the coming of spring. He could smell fresh earth and new grass, could feel the caressing wind on his cheek. All at once he remembered how fine it had felt, as a child in Toronto, to open his coat and run towards the wind which cooled his chest. There had been bells in those days and the smell of hot-buttered popcorn, the shine of red glazed taffy on new apples, and the sound of the peanut vendor's whistle in the time after supper when children ran free on light feet and grownups called peaceably to one another across the broad untravelled streets.

His vision seemed to flutter and tremble. The person facing him had now placed himself fully in the bedchamber, wrapped in his aureole, ready to make some precious communication. His hair, worn loose and flowing almost to his shoulders, was now lifted slightly and moved in the circulating air currents. His sleeves too, broad and cleverly ornamented with embroidered patterns, pulsed with the movement of the air. There was some change coming in the quality of the illumination, like the alteration at the beginning of a film or play when the figures in the action are picked out and emphasised by deliberate plotting of light sources. His head and shoulders came into precise focus and a darkening took place at the skirts of his robe. The elegant sandals or slippers he wore, with elaborately ornamented tips to their toes, became less visible, became more details in his dress than points for some concentration of attention. Had there been little bells suspended from the curled tips of the toes? Was the person in some sort of motley? This seemed unlikely, but the comically tipped shoes or slippers gave the moment an air of the funny, of gaiety, which disallowed impertinent solemnity. This was certainly not to be a solemn event. If anything, quite the reverse.

Bells, the sound of small bells, seemed appropriate to the moment. It struck Neil that his otherwise soundless and voiceless visitor was accompanied by faint tinklings like the sounding of the triangle in an Italian symphony. Perhaps these chimings originated in the movement of the wind across roofs, through bell towers into dreamers' bedchambers. Bells, tinklings. The visionary visitor carried a stringed instrument, a cithern or some other primitive version of the guitar. The instrument was long-necked, six-stringed, made of wooden inlay inset in complex patterns recalling the work of Boulle. Gold and black lacquer, taut waxy yellow strings.

Many of the great Venetian painters had been skilful musicians he realised. Perhaps this person was about to play for him; the instrument was slung from his shoulders in a position suitable for ready performance. The late-night visitor followed his gaze, observed his fascination with the instrument, seemed momentarily to ready it for playing, then smiled a trifle forlornly and laid his cithern against his hip. He seemed unable to speak or produce any sound. Was the cithern a merely symbolic property meant to lend authenticity to this experience? The product of a dreaming imagination? If so, which of them was dreaming? Neil opened and shut his eyes rapidly several times. He was certain he was wide awake but he all at once remembered having had many dreams in which he had been sure he was as wide awake as now. If a dream were vivid enough it would be impossible to distinguish it from waking. He could readily dream of pain, even sharp pain, so pinching himself wasn't a definitive test. He might hurl himself from the window to fall into the canal. It wasn't possible to dream the experience of falling from a height into chill water. Or was it? He decided not to try.

The night visitor turned his eyes directly towards Neil with an entreating gaze, a rolling of the eyes which just missed being comic. There was an extremely Venetian expressiveness to this movement of the eyes, a pathetic earnestness – more than earnestness – entreaty, supplication, which preserved the friendly air of his regard, its quality of high good humour, at the same time signalling mental discomfort and apprehension. Neil had seen this same expression in a thousand paintings of mythological and religious subjects, a sidewise-turning, slanting subtle gaze which communicated a sense of comic secrets shared: participation in the arranged elopement of two young couples, reception of some young and valued guest. Often the happy angels of Venetian painting shared their religious intuitions with the same slanting exulting glance. Venetian too was the midnight conspiratorial secrecy of the encounter. He and the other might be characters in one of the celebrated Venetian libretti, set by Vivaldi for performance in the not very distant opera house.

Discourse must be established between them but in what way? Neil couldn't decipher the language of light, the pulsings and moving striations of the apparition's halo. They were surely the forms of expression of a phantom language but what did they mean? How respond to them? He stared more and more ardently at the young man who approached him and tried to speak. His lips moved, his eyes sparkled, one arm caressed the cithern, the other was raised in a pleading motion.

"What do you want?" gasped Neil. "Who are you?"

The features of the deeply compelled young man contorted in an agony of mute expression, a plea – but what was asked? What response would satisfy? He was a handsome young man, well above medium height and strongly built, a courtly man, that much was plain. When he moved he almost danced with a courtier's grace or the expressive motion and grace of a richly-endowed actor. Neil had seen Sir Laurence Olivier move like that. There was a hint of Olivier in the young man's looks, in the eyes and the carrying of the head. Was he an actor? An artist of some sort? Musician? Painter? As this last guess crossed Neil's imagination the face of his visitor was lit up with a vast kindly glow, a painter, of course, the stringed instrument and dancing movements were false clues. Now the apparition gave Neil a brilliant and reassuring smile.

A darkly handsome young man, an amateur of music, richly dressed, strongly built, a native of the Veneto, victim of some agonising distress, exhilarated by possession of extraordinary gifts. Perhaps a painter. This could only be the treasured intimate of Cardinal Bembo, the youth possessed of all the talents, every endowment of mind and body, the adored leader of his circle, confidant of Leonardo himself.

But he never existed, Neil thought, there never was such a person. And at this momentary lapse of faith, he saw the ghostly form shrivel and start and grow wan, his light attenuated, his clothes flat and limp about him. Once more an extreme agitation showed in his gaze, this time unmistakeably a prayer, a beseeching. Neil's mind vibrated with a communication he had not thought possible to receive. No such message could ever be sent, he had thought, for it had no source, no sender.

Creak, creak, went the frames of the wide-open windows as the wind rushed around corners and through crevices. The night was ending. Neil tried to get up. He propped himself against the fat pillows and swung his legs towards the side of the bed but his guest anticipated the movement and flung out his right arm in a gesture of restraint, coming much closer to the hangings of the bed and its framing boards. Was he about to kneel? He made as if to set aside the musical instrument which encumbered him but Neil completed his own movement, sat up and turned to rise. The visitor began to draw back, the broad bands of light which framed him growing narrower, paler. Neil felt his bare feet touch the chilly floor. He was unquestionably awake and in full possession of his senses. The figure was still plainly visible, man-sized, begging, darkening, contorting itself into a painful posture of uncommunicated desire.

"Tell me what you want. Speak to me!"

Only the sound of the wind and the currents of lagoon and canal.

"Don't go! Speak to me! I'll do whatever you want!"

Then, as the figure retreated towards the window, there came a

66

moment of calm and arrest in which the sound of the wind and the water seemed to fade from Neil's hearing. His night visitor, a friend, an intimate he felt sure, a person who would live forever in his heart, stood erect and tranquil, let his arms hang peacefully at his sides, smiled at him acceptingly, consolingly and stepped away backwards and again backwards to the small balcony which lay behind him. His enclosing circle of light dimmed and disappeared, and his outline became shadowy and indistinct in the beginnings of a blue dawn and then he vanished.

Feeling that he must rest or be tormented forever by anxieties and indecisions, Neil stumbled back to his bed, fell upon it in a lover's embrace, wound the bedclothes around himself in a protective cocoon and relapsed into a profound sleep.

The sun was high in the shining sky when he awoke. Attenuated shadows told him that the time was close to noon. He had a lot to do: Pack his bag, sink his documents in the canal, return the typewriter. This would take considerable time. He bundled and cramped all his material relating to his recent research into a large plastic carry-all which he'd been using in his work. By dint of much compression the entire stock of heavy paper was squashed down into a space about the size of a cardboard carton from any neighbourhood grocery store. *Let it all go. I'll proceed no further in this business.*

Photocopies, slides, colour reproductions – all. In half-an-hour he had prepared the work of years for destruction. He shaved, dressed, gathered his money and traveller's cheques, stood eager for departure. Taking a last look around his room he noticed a scrap of stiff paper lying near his bed. He saw that it formed part of the altarpiece documentation, the single manuscript word "ZanZan." The only clear writing on the paper.

He tore this single scrap into confetti, strode to the window and out onto the little false balcony. There he committed the tiny bits of paper to the swimming air. A storm of fluttering paper snow spread across the roofs of Venice. Pigeons circled, saw that the flakes were inedible, turned away. Neil closed the windows, took up his belongings and left the room. In the entryway to the pensione he secured the devout promises of his host and hostess

67

that they would faithfully carry out the task of destruction assigned to them, sinking his load of papers in the nearby canal some dark night. Neil had no doubt they would do as he asked; a perfectly genuine friendship existed among them and he might someday return to Venice as tourist or sightseer.

He stepped into the Campo Santa Margherita for a final visit. Diagonally across the square was the stationery store where he had meant to make his blowups. No need of their technical help now; an emissary from the Pensione Due Foscari would return his rented typewriter and settle the small account. The sight of the neat doorway, the window display of sophisticated machinery, troubled him deeply, plumbed some hitherto uninvestigated depth of conscience from whose recesses nothing profitable was apt to emerge. He retreated from this vision of high-tech communication towards the canal where he immediately found a gondolier idling at the landing stage below the neighbouring bridge.

In a few moments they were headed towards the railway station by way of the Rio Nuovo. It was during this brief time of transit from pensione to railway car that Neil realised a great weight had been lifted from his bowed shoulders, a load which yesterday had seemed old and heavy as winter. Soon it would be April. On Woodlawn, Walker, and Alcorn Avenues – and on Yonge Street – the crowds of young men and women would be flocking towards their equivalent of the Rialto, the Nag's Head pub. Soothed by the gentle motion of his gondola, Neil sorted over his feelings and saw that he was extraordinarily pleased to be on his way home. Refreshment and a strange charmed release of tension had arrived with his midnight visitor. A great weight of responsibility might now be surrendered. He didn't have the temperament of a revisionist. He couldn't bring himself to undeceive so many, to substitute informed historical reasoning and proof for legend and fantastic imagining.

Only a superbly prideful man will undertake to expunge legend from history. He thought of the great and famous saints – Saint George, Saint Christopher – whose very names had been banished from the calendar together with their *cultus,* by shortsighted investigators who based revisionism upon mere fact.

What humble suppliant, eager for the intercession of the saint before the heavenly throne, would gladly receive the assurance that the saint whose aid he implored was nothing but a pious figment of superstition?

You don't meddle with peoples' dreams. The gondola bumped against the sloping quayside. Here stood the railway station. Here he took his farewell of the many-islanded republic. In a few minutes he had obtained a place on the noon service to Milan. There would be time at the end of the day to book a new reservation for the direct Milan-Toronto flight. This wasn't even the shoulder of the season; there would be no problem altering his date of departure. He drew a small notebook from an inner pocket to make notes about his peculiar experience the previous night. He wondered about the manifold specific details which the experience had presented to his attention: the precision of the visual imagery, the unbelievable accuracy and *presence* of the golden and silver and crimson threads of embroidery on the sleeves of his visitor's cope or cloak. Where had it all come from? Was it simply a brilliant collage of impressions recorded and preserved in his fancies in the course of the last months, offered up to the demands of a fatigued and heated brain?

He shifted uneasily in his seat as the train began to move, remembering that in his bed, moving uneasily in a state of confusion, he hadn't been able to decide whether he was asleep or awake. Was he going to be left in this anxious dilemma for some time, perhaps forever? Of course not. He could always finally distinguish sleep from waking. All the entrancing things happened when he was asleep. The boring, the ugly, the dull obligations were never encountered in dreams or great works of art. Palma, Sebastiano, Lorenzo, Giovanni, Tiziano, I salute you, he thought, as the train gained the far shore and changed its motion. And you most of all, my friend of the late night, my San Giorgio.

And with this happy resolve he felt relieved of care. His heart rose. There were other undertakings ahead. He would look up his friends in Toronto to tell them about his adventures, losing nothing in the telling. He would play Marco Polo to their astonished stay-at-homes, bring out one fantastic jewel after another, more and more rich gifts from the Great Khan, scents and colours never smelled nor seen in the Nag's Head.

The daytime flight from Milan leaves a little before noon. On Alitalia, it takes just under eight hours to make the crossing and arrive 3:00 PM Toronto time. Travelling light, one-bagging it, Neil easily caught the bus downtown to the Royal York terminus, where he boarded the subway uptown to the Summerhill station. He never occupied himself overmuch with the trivialities of departure and return, never expected to be met at the airport and, in fact, never was. Nobody in the air terminal. Nobody at the Royal York. He saw nobody he knew in the Summerhill subway station, nobody during the short distance from Yonge Street to Walker Avenue. Dust around the doorframe of the apartment, dust in his halls, a fine sifting overlying his gallery of coloured reproductions – those would come down soon – and traceable impressions of the motions of the air in the dust on kitchen counters. He started the refrigerator which smelled fresh and sweet despite his four months' absence. He might go out and do a bit of grocery shopping later on at the all-night deli around the corner.

The flat seemed unaffected by prolonged absence. It struck him as having the air of a museum reproduction of a period style: Imagine some lady docent standing in front of a three-sided re-creation of these living quarters reciting from a scenario.

The home of an educated professional worker of the late twentieth century, evidently a person of refined taste and breeding if we are to judge by the preoccupation with fine art suggested by the decoration of the rooms. The convenience of arrangements for the preparation of food and drink gives us a clue to the marital status of the subject who almost certainly lived alone. There is but a single bedroom in which a collection of native artifacts is displayed, and in other rooms cheap copies of more celebrated works from other cultures were given pride of place. This man or woman was deeply unsure of the values of his or her society; at the same time, there was a reluctance to abandon them in favour of a problematic historicism.

Thus the archaeologist of the year 2385.

It was all true. He was celibate, from choice as much as from accident. There were inescapable problems in his life at this very moment but he felt that he was on the verge of dismissing them forever. No point in wedding oneself to the past in the way the Doges had attempted to marry the surging turbulent Adriatic. He went around the apartment drawing back curtains and throwing open windows. Gusts of air, not the marine winds of the salt sea, more the gasoline fumes of Yonge Street, began to circulate along his corridors.

Smog, he thought, inhaling happily.

He looked at his wristwatch and saw that he had made extraordinarily good time from the airport to his home; it was barely 5.00. Happy hour, he thought, feeling an impulse to giggle. He remembered that happy hour was illegal in Toronto.

There was no sound in the building. Thoughts of happy hour naturally brought imaginings of the Nag's Head to mind. That was where his friends and acquaintances would be. He suddenly felt a great need to see Betty Frits, not for her sexual charms – which though distinct and actual were not her principal assets – but because of her homey familiarity. Maybe she had some assignment for him which would pay a modest honorarium while reacquainting him with local problems in art history.

Of course, she did. She was the first person he spotted upon his arrival at the old watering-hole. She was standing down at the end of the bar among a crowd of companions, absorbed in recounting some adventure of the Toronto legal and corporate world. Snatches of terminology drifted towards Neil. "... escrow ... public trustee ... non-refundable contributions." She caught sight of him and her eyes brightened.

She isn't such a bad looking dame after all, Neil said to himself in studied parody. She came over and drew him into the very same booth in which some months before they had drifted into the deep waters of Renaissance ascription.

"Got a job for you, and I've persuaded the firm to raise its rates. We can do you $800 *per diem* or $500 for a half-day's consultancy."

"How long should it take?"

She nudged him under the ribs. "Just as long as you consider necessary."

"I'm on salary at the university. I'm not an indigent."

She said, "I know that, but a little of what you fancy does you good. Correct?"

"Tell me about it."

"It's a lady whose family has always given us its wills and executorships. She has this painting, a big one. She's trying to convince herself it's an A.Y. Jackson. The market for A.Y.'s work is soft just now, but a painting of this size, about 3' x 4', large for a Jackson, now and then sells for as much as $20,000. Naturally she'd like to know if it's for real."

"But she's afraid it's really by Fred Banting."

"Oh, you know about that?"

"They used to go on painting trips together. Eventually Doctor Banting got so he did a pretty good Jackson imitation. Is the work signed?"

"Signed by Jackson but, personally, I'd be prepared to swear the signature's a forgery."

Neil took a long swallow from the stein which Betty passed to him. "I'll run a few tests," he said. "A couple of days should do it."

"Let's hope you come up with an affirmative judgment."

"I expect I will." He took a second deep draught and then almost strangled as a broad palm smote him between the shoulder blades in mid-swallow. Gasping and choking he turned to face his assailant.

"Take that, pardner," said Huey-Jack DuBoys.

"You trying to kill me, big guy?"

"Shuckins, no, jest glad to see you, buddy. Listen up now, I want you to tell me, did you rewrite any little ole history while you were off in them furrin' parts? You find out anythang?"

Neil looked from Huey-Jack to Betty and back. He wiped his mouth and chin.

"No," he said, "I found nothing."